"Wulff, help me—please," she pleaded.

In a moment he was holding her. "Of course I will, girl. I'll help you. But you have to let me know what you want from me. I don't understand—"

Brittany looked up into his handsome face, only inches from hers. His warm breath fanned her cheek. She could feel the hard swell of the muscles in his arms which were wrapped tightly around her waist.

She watched as her own arms wound around his neck, her palm gliding over the tiny wisps of hair that curled over his shirt collar.

At that moment she knew exactly what she wanted from Aren Wulff. Lifting her lips toward his, she tangled her fingers in his thick, dark hair and pulled his head down to hers.

Dear Reader,

Spellbinders! That's what we're striving for. The editors at Silhouette are determined to capture your imagination and win your heart with every single book we publish. Each month, six Special Editions are chosen with *you* in mind.

Our authors are our inspiration. Writers such as Nora Roberts, Tracy Sinclair, Kathleen Eagle, Carole Halston and Linda Howard—to name but a few—are masters at creating endearing characters and heartrending love stories. Their characters are everyday people—just like you and me—whose lives have been touched by love, whose dream and desire suddenly comes true!

So find a cozy, quiet place to read, and create your own special moment with a Silhouette Special Edition.

Sincerely,

Rosalind Noonan
Senior Editor
SILHOUETTE BOOKS

SONJA MASSIE
Legacy of the Wolf

Silhouette Special Edition

Published by Silhouette Books New York

America's Publisher of Contemporary Romance

Dedicated to
Lady Gwendolynn,
Prince Arden
and
King Arthur,
who loved a simple maiden . . .
and made her his queen

The author would like to thank Terry Bridwell
for his nautical expertise, which contributed so much
to this novel.

SILHOUETTE BOOKS
300 East 42nd St., New York, N.Y. 10017

Copyright © 1986 by Sonja Massie

ISBN: 0-373-09348-9

First Silhouette Books printing November 1986

America's Publisher of Contemporary Romance

Printed in the U.S.A.

SONJA MASSIE

lives in Southern California with her husband, two children, dog, cat, bunny and cockatiel. After numerous careers and business undertakings, she has finally decided "what she wants to be when she grows up"—a writer. Silhouette is proud to introduce her first novel in our Special Edition line.

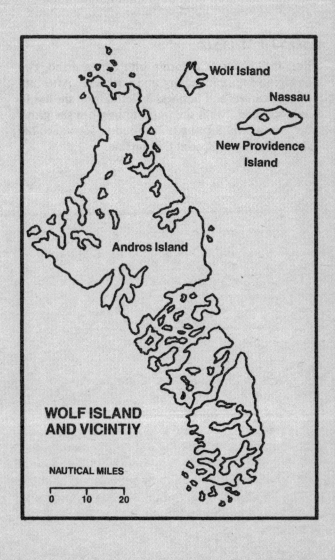

Wolf Island

Nassau

New Providence
Island

Andros Island

WOLF ISLAND
AND VICINTIY

NAUTICAL MILES

0   10   20

Chapter One

Brittany Davis stared up into the palest blue eyes that she had ever seen. They seemed to peer into her very soul and see things that, at least for the time being, she wanted to keep hidden from the world. Not the whole world, she thought, just the people on this tiny Bahamian island.

"Who is this man?" she asked the red-haired girl who stood behind the counter in the small, but well-stocked general store.

"What man?" the girl asked, squeezing through the narrow space between the end of the counter and a bunch of bananas that hung from a hook on the wall. Her progress was hindered by her enlarged abdomen. She was obviously very young... and very pregnant.

"The incredibly handsome man in this painting," Brittany replied.

The little shopkeeper padded over to stand beside Brittany beneath the painting that hung on the back wall of the store near a display of straw hats.

"Oh, that's Captain Jonathan Wulff. He was our first lighthouse keeper." The girl folded her hands over the bulk of her stomach and leaned back against a table covered with batik printed shirts.

"He and his family were shipwrecked on the rocks in Wolf Cove, but they survived. They fell in love with the island and decided to settle here. Captain Wulff had the lighthouse built there in 1859 to warn other sailors away from the rocks that destroyed his ship. He's sort of our island hero."

Brittany tried to swallow the lump that was forming in her throat. "Is that why you have his picture hanging here in the store?"

"That's one reason." The redhead smiled shyly. "The other is because he's pretty to look at, don't you think?"

"He is indeed," Brittany replied grudgingly as she admired the thick mane of chestnut hair that surrounded the captain's lean, rugged face.

His neatly trimmed black beard and mustache, and the angular planes of his face gave the impression of masculine severity. But his remarkable blue eyes shone with a warmth that she hadn't expected to see in Captain Jonathan Wulff's gaze.

"So, that's Captain Wulff," she muttered. A wave of anger swept over her, leaving her knees weak.

"Oh, you've heard of him?"

"Ah, yes."

"I'm sorry. I didn't mean to bore you with the island's history."

"That's okay," Brittany replied dryly. "This island's history is far from boring. Tell me, is Wolf Lighthouse still operating?"

"It sure is. As a matter of fact, the keeper is Captain Wulff's great-grandson, Aren Wulff." A shy grin spread across her freckled cheeks. "He looks just like the captain, if you know what I mean."

"Pretty to look at, huh?"

The girl nodded vigorously, causing her copper curls to bob. "Yep, but we don't see him very often. He stays to himself most of the time. It's a lot of work, keeping a lighthouse."

"Does he live all alone up there?"

"Yeah, but my cousin, Bob, is his assistant. And my little brother, Jesse, is always hanging around pestering Mr. Wulff. He's teaching Jesse how to read," she said proudly.

"Don't you have a school here on the island?"

"No. The big islands do, but it's too far to take the kids to Andros every day. We get along all right. Jesse says that after Mr. Wulff teaches him how to read, Jesse will teach me. Grandma taught me numbers so that I could run the store now that she's too old. But I'd like to be able to read really good, you know, books and stuff."

"Well, with your enthusiasm I'm sure you'll learn very quickly. How old is Jesse?" Brittany asked as she resumed her shopping around the tiny store. She picked up two oranges and a bottle of lemon-lime soda.

"He's seven, nine years younger than me."

Only sixteen. Brittany's eyes slid down to the girl's belly, then glanced quickly away.

The little redhead's freckled cheeks blushed a pale pink as she followed Brittany's gaze. "This last winter

I went to Nassau," she said softly, staring at the worn, wooden-planked floor. "I got a job working in a restaurant there. We needed the money really bad, me and Grandma and Jesse. Grandma told me that I shouldn't go. She said that I was too young to take care of myself. I guess she was right, huh?"

Brittany didn't answer, but studied the amber eyes that continued to stare at the floor, not meeting hers. The fear and shame that she saw there pulled at her heartstrings. She had seen that same lost, frightened look in the eyes of too many pregnant teenagers.

"Looks like your baby's about due. Who's going to help with your delivery? Is there a doctor on the island?"

"No. The nearest doctor is in Nicholl's Town on Andros. It's eight miles south. Mr. Wulff said that he'll take me over there in his boat when my time comes. He took Jesse to the clinic there last year when he fell out of a tree and broke his arm. I'm not too scared, really. If there's an emergency my grandma can help me out. She's delivered babies before. It's just that she's getting so old."

The girl's thin shoulders drooped, as though they carried the weight of the world. Brittany resisted the urge to put her arms around her. Instead, she said, "I'd be glad to help you in any way I can. I'm a registered nurse."

"Really? Oh, that's good." She breathed a sigh of relief. "I'm glad that you'll be around, just in case. But are you going to be staying? I thought you were just a tourist who's passing through."

"I'll be staying if I can find a place to live. Do you know anyone who might have a room to rent for a few weeks?"

"I sure do. We have a little cabin out behind our house. It's not very big, but it's clean and it's right on the beach. You could rent that if my grandma says it's okay. I'm sure she will. We can really use the money."

"Great. Let me pay for these things, and I'll go speak to her about it."

"I'd better take you down to the house later, after I close up the store. Grandma's taking her afternoon nap right now, and she gets really grumpy if you wake her up."

"Well, I certainly wouldn't want to do that. By the way—" Brittany extended her hand to the girl "—if I'm going to be your neighbor, I should introduce myself. I'm Brittany Davis."

Timidly shaking Brittany's outstretched hand, the girl replied, "Hi, I'm Debra Wilson. Welcome to Wolf Island. It's a beautiful place. You'll have a lot of fun here."

A shadow flitted across Brittany's face. "Thank you," she replied. "Tell me, how do people get around on this island? Looks like most of them are either walking or riding bikes."

"That's how we do it," the girl replied as she brushed a stray curl out of her eyes. "There are only a couple of motorbikes on the island, and the owners have a hard time getting fuel for those. Why? Where do you want to go?"

"Well, since I've got a couple of hours to spare, I think I'll go up to Wolf Lighthouse and see if the keeper will show me around."

"I have a bicycle that's not getting much use these days for obvious reasons," Debra said, patting her belly. "If you'd like to use it while you're here, you're welcome to."

"Thank you. I promise to take good care of it."

Debra snickered and said, "Don't worry about that. You can't hurt the old thing. It was trashed when I got it. In fact, I think it's been on the island since Christopher Columbus sailed through here. I just hope it doesn't fall apart under you." She shuffled uneasily from one foot to the other. "But you know, if I were you, I wouldn't go up to the lighthouse. I'm afraid Mr. Wulff doesn't have much patience with tourists."

"Really? Well, I guess I'll have to take my chances."

"I'll tell you what." Debra rummaged under the counter and then handed a small box of fuses to Brittany. "Mr. Wulff ordered these a couple of weeks ago and I got them this morning. He said to let him know as soon as they came in. I was going to have Jesse take them up to him, but if you're going, you could take them along. Tell him that I asked you to deliver them for me."

Brittany slipped the box into her shirt pocket. "Do you really think he'll believe that?"

A broad smile sliced through the freckles on Debra's face. "No. But if he's in a good mood, he might pretend to."

As Brittany bumped along the narrow dirt road, she managed to guide Debra's bicycle around most of the mud holes left by last night's storm. The thick brush on either side of the road steamed in the tropical sun, turning the island into a giant sauna.

The only relief from the heat and humidity came from the steady breeze that blew off the ocean. The gentle wind quickly whipped Brittany's waist-long blond hair into a tangle, making her wish that she had thought to tie it back before she had begun her ride.

Stopping for a moment to wipe the beads of perspiration from her forehead, she surveyed the road ahead and hoped that the end would soon be in sight. Brittany considered herself to be physically fit, but the road was steep and several miles long. Patting the box of fuses in her pocket she pushed off again.

Just when she thought her trembling legs were going to surrender the battle, she saw it: the end of the road and a gray stone wall with a white gate. A sign, shaped like a wolf's head, hung from an arch over the gate. The animal's mouth was open and its fangs were bared menacingly. It reminded her of signs that she had seen hanging outside British pubs and taverns.

She had found Wolf Light.

Her heart pounded from more than mere exertion. She thoroughly dreaded the coming meeting with Aren Wulff. So much depended on it. She had to make a good impression and persuade him to spend some time with her, so she could find out what she needed to know.

Lost in her thoughts and apprehension, Brittany failed to see a small boy chasing a tiny black-and-white puppy through the bushes at the side of the road until the puppy darted directly in front of her.

Swerving hard to the left to avoid hitting them, she fell over on her side in the mud.

"Christopher, look what you did! Now we're in trouble," the boy shouted as he ran to Brittany's side. "I'm sorry, lady. Are you okay?" he asked.

Brittany lay on the damp ground, looking up at a freckled-face tousled-haired boy whom she judged to be about six or seven. For the second time that day she marveled at the unusually brilliant shade of copper-red hair.

Painfully picking herself up, she brushed the mud from her hand to reveal a rather nasty scrape. "I have a feeling that your name is Jesse," she muttered.

"How did you know that?" The boy grabbed the puppy that gamboled unconcerned at his feet.

"I spoke to your sister earlier. She told me that you often come up here to see Mr. Wulff."

"Yeah, I do. He's teaching me how to read. Last month he read *Moby Dick* to me. Someday I'll be able to read it all by myself. He's reading *Treasure Island* to me now."

"That's very nice of him," Brittany reluctantly admitted.

"Mr. Wulff's a nice man. He's going to take Deb to the doctor when she has her baby. It's going to be a boy, you know."

"Is it? How can you be so sure?" she asked, attempting to brush the dirt from her shorts and legs.

"Because that's what I want really, really bad. Having a nephew would be like having a little brother, and I always wanted a brother more than anything in the whole, wide world. And Mr. Wulff says that if you want something more than anything and you don't ever give up hope—someday you'll get it."

"Mr. Wulff says that, huh?" She left the bike at the side of the road and limped toward the gate.

"Yep, that's what he says," the boy replied confidently, trailing at her heels.

"Well, Mr. Wulff is right. That's true. Most of the time," she added, remembering her brother, Michael. Sometimes cruel accidents end people's dreams...and their lives.

"Did you come to see Mr. Wulff?" Jesse asked.

"Yes, I'm bringing some fuses to him." She patted the box in her pocket. "Debra asked me to deliver them. She said that he might not be too friendly, though, because he doesn't like tourists."

"Oh, Deb doesn't know Mr. Wulff as good as I do. He'll be glad to see you." The boy appraised her with a thoroughness beyond his years. "He doesn't like nosy tourists. But he sure likes pretty ladies."

For some reason Brittany thought of the blue eyes in the painting, and a slight chill swept over her. So, he likes ladies. That's good, she thought. I'll use every advantage I have. Whatever it takes . . . for Michael.

Jesse tugged at the heavy gate and gallantly ushered her inside. Together they climbed the steep, stone stairs that led to the front of the light keeper's house.

Larger than the limestone cottages in the village, the house looked as though it had stood for a hundred years and was strong enough to endure yet another century or two.

Nestled against the rock at the base of the lighthouse, the structure reflected a strong New England influence. The walls were built of mortared gray stones and supported a steeply pitched slate roof. The woodwork around the windows and door was painted a glowing white, like the lighthouse that towered above it.

Both were built on the mammoth bluff that comprised Wolf Rock. On the other side of the point lay the sea and a cove filled with craggy rocks—teeth, the teeth of the wolf.

Brittany shuddered to see Wolf Cove for the first time. How could such a beautiful, peaceful place be the scene of so many tragedies?

Jesse seemed to read her thoughts. "That Wolf Cove's a bad place," he said. "Lots of people've smashed their boats and died down there."

"Yes, Jesse, I know," Brittany replied.

As they stepped onto the porch, she spotted a gleaming brass bell over the door. She pulled on its rope and a loud, clear peal filled the air.

Brittany retreated from the door several paces and waited, wishing that her heart would stop its pounding. She tried to smooth her tangled hair with one hand and hid her other dirty bleeding hand behind her. Jesse, seemingly eager to greet the master of the house, pushed in front of her and stood squarely before the door.

Just when Brittany had decided with relief that no one was home, the door opened. There, filling the entryway, was the largest man that she had ever seen.

In an instant she recognized the pale blue eyes and dark chestnut hair that she had found so appealing in the painting. The angular planes of Aren Wulff's face were even more pronounced than his great-grandfather's because he was clean-shaven. Clean-shaven, that is, except for the stubble of overnight growth on his chin and cheeks.

He apparently had been asleep. His hair was uncombed and he wore only a pair of faded jeans.

Brittany's gaze drifted over his massive shoulders and chest, taking in the deeply tanned muscular contours of his torso. In her stomach a pair of butterflies performed a fluttering mating dance and then settled embarrassingly low in her body.

Her eyes trailed down the dark chest hair that narrowed to a line and disappeared into jeans that he had zipped but neglected to snap. Chiding herself for having such a keen interest in his chest and jeans, Brittany forced her eyes upward and studied the man's face.

The keeper shielded his eyes from the bright light with the back of his hand and squinted down at Jesse, who stood smiling eagerly at the sleepy giant they had aroused.

Aren Wulff lowered his hand and ruffled the boy's brassy curls. "Jesse, you flea-bitten little bilge rat, you know that I was up all night with that storm. I ought to hang you from the top of the light by your ears and let the gulls pick off your freckles."

Jesse grinned up at the man, his eyes shining with adoration. Obviously he was unintimidated by the gruesome threat.

"So, what's so important that you hauled me out of my bunk?" the keeper asked.

"I brought you some company." Jesse motioned toward Brittany.

Wulff noticed her for the first time, standing off to the side of the porch behind the boy.

Her body tingled as his blue eyes swept her from head to toe. Slowly, sensuously he evaluated her, even as she had him moments before.

When he finally lifted his gaze to hers, his face was inscrutable. She couldn't tell if he approved of her or not.

His eyes stared into hers with the same intensity that his great-grandfather's had. Brittany had the uncomfortable feeling that in an instant this man knew all of her secrets—all but one. She swallowed hard and started to introduce herself, but Jesse interrupted her.

"This lady was coming up here to see you, but Christopher Columbus ran out in front of her and made her fall off her bike. She hurt her hand pretty bad, see.''

Jesse grabbed Brittany's injured hand and held it out for Wulff's inspection.

"You're going to have to teach that pup of yours some manners, Jess. We can't have him going around knocking ladies off their bikes now, can we?''

Wulff gently took Brittany's hand from Jesse and looked at her red scraped palm. His huge hand was rough, weathered and warm around hers. The rest of him was probably even warmer....

Brittany looked up to see Wulff watching her, a slightly amused look on his handsome features. She felt a fleeting sense of loss when he released her hand. He opened the door wider and stepped back into the house.

"Well, you'd better come inside. Looks like that hand needs some attention.''

Brittany started to explain that her injury wasn't that serious, but quickly stifled her protest, eager to accept any invitation into the house. Silently, she blessed Jesse.

"Thank you, that's very kind of you," she said.

As she swept through the narrow doorway past Wulff, her bare forearm brushed his. The spot on her arm seemed to glow, ignited by the aura of vitality that radiated from him.

Aura? Radiation? Come on, she thought. He's just a man. It's silly to even be conscious of such a brief, casual contact.

But she was.

And what's more, she had the distinct feeling that he was, too.

Jesse and Christopher Columbus followed closely behind her. Without a moment's hesitation, the pup headed straight for the fireplace, where he happily left his damp mark on the gray stone hearth.

Wulff growled and picked the puppy up by the scruff of his neck. Holding him out to Jesse, he said, "I think you'd better clean that up and take Christopher outside before I make a spotted rug out of him."

Jesse snickered. "He's too little to make a rug out of. There's not enough of him."

"Well, I was figuring on using part of his master's speckled hide to make up the difference," Wulff threatened.

Jesse's brown eyes darted knowingly from Wulff to Brittany. "Come on, Chris. We know when we're not wanted."

He took the cloth that Wulff tossed him and cleaned the puddle. Tucking the puppy under his arm, he headed for the door. He cast another glance at Brittany and said to Wulff, "Now don't you get too busy and forget our reading time."

Wulff grinned and swatted the boy playfully on the rear. "I won't forget. Now run along."

After closing the door behind Jesse, he turned to Brittany. "Well, girl, I'll get some antiseptic for that hand of yours."

Resenting the fact that he had referred to her as a girl, Brittany raised herself to her full five feet, seven inches and said pointedly, "My name is Brittany."

One corner of his mouth twitched and his eyes sparkled. "So it is," he replied. "I'm Aren Wulff. I'll shake your hand—after it's clean."

In the corner of the living room stood a large mahogany cupboard with leaded glass doors. He unlocked it and took out a white case with a red cross emblazoned on the lid.

Brittany watched him out of the corner of her eye, trying not to notice the extraordinary breadth of his shoulders or the way his closely fitted faded jeans rode so tantalizingly low on his hips. His slender, firm hips. She forced her eyes upward.

On one set of bulging biceps he wore a vivid tattoo of a wolf's head. Shaped like the sign over the gate, the wolf's mouth was open and its pointed fangs were bared.

For a few brief moments she allowed herself to fantasize, her hand exploring the hardness of his biceps, her fingertip tracing the outline of the tattoo, his skin warm and smooth. . . .

Why hadn't he put on a shirt before he answered the door?

She lifted her gaze to study his face. If she couldn't keep her eyes off him, at least she would keep them off his body.

His softly curled chestnut mane silently invited her fingers to wander through its thickness even as his dusting of beard beckoned her to explore its texture.

The hours he had spent in the Caribbean sun registered on his bronzed skin and the tiny laugh lines around his eyes. A hint of gray sprinkled the wisps that curled over his temples.

She judged that he must be around forty, maybe a bit more.

Wulff took the case to a round oak dining table at the end of the living room. He gave her a sideways glance and grinned when he saw her eyes on his torso. She looked quickly away and felt a crimson flush stain her cheeks.

As though reading her thoughts, he chuckled and reached for a white cotton shirt that hung on the back of a chair. He slipped into it, but to her dismay and delight, he neglected to button the front.

"Have a seat over here," he said, pointing to one of the ladder-back chairs at the table.

Brittany looked down at the mud on her shorts. "I'd better stand. I'll get your chair dirty."

"That's all right. It's seen dirt in its day," he replied.

She sat down as he pulled another chair next to hers and lowered his bulk into it. He leaned alarmingly close to her, filling her senses with his overwhelming presence.

"So, let's see it," he said, holding out his giant hand to her. She couldn't help noticing how small and white her hand looked lying in his rough, warm palm. He held it lightly, turning it over as he examined the scrape.

"Just as I thought," he said, his voice deep and suspiciously grave. "We're going to have to amputate."

Surprised, Brittany glanced up at him and saw the teasing sparkle in his blue eyes. "Aren't you going to give me an anesthetic?" she asked solemnly.

"Sure, I keep it handy for all my serious surgeries." He reached across to the center of the table and picked up a bottle of rum and a small tumbler. He poured a half a glassful of the amber fluid and slid it in front of her. "There you go, girl, fine Caribbean rum. It's the best anesthetic that there is for scraped palms, broken hearts and shattered dreams."

Pain flashed across Brittany's face. She pushed the glass away as though it were poison. "I don't drink. Not anymore," she stated firmly.

Wulff was quiet for a moment before continuing. "Okay then, I don't have any bullets for you to bite on, so you'll have to grit your teeth and hang on . . . to me if you like," he added, grinning.

An unwilling smile curled her lips. "That's okay," she replied huskily, "I'm tough."

Carefully he covered the abrasion with an antiseptic cream. His callused fingertips slowly circled her palm, tracing the lines, the heel of her hand, the base of her thumb. They gently probed the ultrasensitive shadowed areas between her fingers.

Brittany squirmed on her chair. Since when had her palm been connected to the more intimate, feminine parts of her body?

Wulff lowered her hand to her lap and left the room. A moment later he returned with a bowl of water. He placed it on the table and sat down.

Lifting her hand, he dipped it into the warm water. She gasped softly.

"I'm sorry," he said, his voice deep and soothing. "I'll bet that smarts."

"It's okay," she replied hoarsely.

Her hand was fine. It was the rest of her that was on fire.

She sighed, closed her eyes and inhaled the masculine scent of his body. She could feel herself melting, submitting to the light keeper's hands, hands that were so big and yet incredibly gentle.

With a piece of gauze he carefully washed away every trace of the cream and dirt. Then he lifted her hand from the bowl and patted it dry with a soft white towel. He laid her hand, palm up, on his thigh.

The heat from his leg filtered through the worn denim, warming the back of her hand. Yes, his thigh was every bit as hard as it looked.

Wulff took a roll of gauze from the white case and wound a few strips around her hand. "There," he said as he fastened it with some surgical tape. "That wasn't so bad, now was it?"

Brittany flexed her hand and admired the bandaging. "It wasn't bad at all. You did a good job, if I do say so myself. Almost as good as I would have done."

"Oh, is that right?" he asked, lifting one eyebrow. "Are you some kind of authority on bandaging?"

"Sort of," she replied. "I'm a nurse."

His eyes widened slightly, and he surveyed her with renewed respect. "Well, I'll be damned. You might have mentioned that my technique was being evaluated by an expert."

"Why? Your technique is fine. And so is your bedside manner," she added, remembering his gentleness.

The instant the words had escaped her mouth, Brittany wanted to recall them. She glanced up at him to see if he was thinking along the same lines that she was. His eyes flashed, and the corner of his mouth once again pulled into a grin.

"Now, what would you be knowing, girl, about my technique or my bedside manners?"

She cleared her throat nervously. "You—you know what I meant," she stammered.

"Yeah, I do. I was just having some fun with you."

He turned to pack the gauze and antiseptic back into the case. "So, tell me, Nurse Brittany, what are you doing on Wolf Island? Why did you come up to see me this morning? And why do I feel like I know you?"

She chose the one question for which she had an answer. "I was in Debra's store this morning, and we were talking about your great-grandfather's picture. Then we discussed the lighthouse and I told her that I'm fascinated by lighthouses."

"And how do you feel about lighthouse keepers?" he asked, grinning mischievously as he eyed her full lower lip.

"Well, to date I've only met one. But based on my limited knowledge, I'd say that they bandage hands very well and are a bit forward with the ladies."

Wulff laughed. "Well, I guess I deserved that."

Brittany reached into her shirt pocket and produced the box of fuses. "Debra told me that you ordered these. She said that they're important, so I offered to bring them up to you."

Wulff took the box from her and looked directly into her eyes, searching, questioning.

Brittany tried her best to return his level gaze. Unpracticed in the art of deception, she found that she couldn't, and dropped her eyes.

"Thank you," he muttered, placing the box into his shirt pocket. Then he added lightly, "If I'd known that Debra had hired you as a delivery boy, I'd have ordered the fuses sooner. Now for my other questions. Why are you here on Wolf Island? We don't get many tourists, especially during the hurricane season."

Shifting nervously in her chair, Brittany cursed herself for not having prepared answers to these questions. She should have known he would ask them.

"I, uh, I didn't know that it was hurricane season. I was vacationing in Nassau when someone told me about Wolf Island. They told me some of its history, and I thought I would come over and explore a bit."

"And what chapter of our illustrious past did you find so fascinating that you strayed from the tourist-beaten path? Blockade-running, rum-running, piracy, drug running?"

"The blockade-runners," she answered cautiously. She took a deep breath. "And moon cursers."

Wulff lifted one eyebrow in surprise. "Now, why would a nice girl like you be interested in those bloody devils?"

"They're a morbid subject and, you must admit, morbid subjects are usually fascinating," she replied evenly.

"I guess that's true. But how do you know the term moon cursers? Most non islanders call them wreckers, if they know about them at all."

"That's what the fellow called them who told me about them... the guy in Nassau."

"Right," Wulff replied. The twinkle left his eyes and their clear blue clouded with suspicion. "So, why did you come up here? Do you want to find out about lighthouses or moon cursers?"

"Both," she replied, "if you have time and don't mind."

Wulff carefully studied the young woman who sat at his table. She was a pretty sight with waves of thick, luxurious hair spilling over her shoulders. His fingers itched to touch it. He couldn't help wondering if those golden curls felt as silky as they looked.

And her eyes, so full of pain and guilt. Unusual topaz eyes framed with long, dark lashes. Where had he seen eyes like those before?

Instinctively, he knew that she had told him nothing but lies since she had arrived. But for some reason he couldn't bring himself to call her on it. She seemed so delicate, so fragile.

He felt the overpowering need to protect her. He wasn't sure from what. But protectiveness wasn't the only overpowering need he was feeling at the moment. Desires that he thought he had under control were asserting themselves with alarming urgency.

Even the simple act of washing her hand had excited him far more than was reasonable. It had been years since he had reacted this acutely to a woman. In fact, he couldn't remember for sure if he ever had.

She was probably trouble. He should send her packing right now. If she stayed...

His eyes strayed to her slender, but well-rounded figure and on down to her long, shapely legs. She was young and obviously vulnerable. Yes, he should definitely send her packing. But Wulff knew himself pretty well...and he knew he wouldn't.

Settling back into his chair, he buttoned his shirt and ran his fingers through his mussed hair. He reached for the glass of rum that she had refused.

"I have the time and I don't mind showing you around. Let's understand one thing up front. This is a sight-seeing trip and not a treasure hunt. Okay? There's no wrecker's stash on this island."

"How can you be so sure?" she asked.

"I'm sure because I spent the first thirty-five years of my life looking for abandoned wrecker's treasure here on Wolf Island. And I can tell you that there isn't any. I know every inch of this island like the back of my hand: every cave, rock and cay. There's nothing here of any monetary value to anybody."

He drained the glass of rum with one swallow and continued. "You know, Nurse Brittany, over the years

I've guided scores of starry-eyed treasure hunters, and you don't strike me as the average pie-in-the-sky fortune seeker."

Brittany dropped her eyes and stared at his hands. "We all have our dreams," she said softly.

"Yes, well, I've felt a lot better since I've given up on a few of mine. Like finding a cave full of gold and..."

"And," she prompted.

His eyes moved slowly over her hair and on down her figure. He cleared his throat and looked out the window. "And a few other elusive fantasies. There's no point in tormenting yourself, I always say."

Brittany watched the play of emotions on his face, intrigued by the various facets of his personality. One minute he flirted and teased; the next moment he seemed lost in the depths of some personal conflict.

He sighed and again raked his fingers through his hair. "So, you'd like to see Wolf Light, huh? I charge quite a bit for a personally guided tour. Are you sure you can afford it?" His teasing smile had returned.

"I don't know," she responded carefully, "I don't have a lot of cash with me."

"That's okay," he said. Again his eyes traced her generous lips. "I'm sure we can work something out."

An icy shiver trickled down Brittany's spine. Whether it came from fear or anticipation, she couldn't tell.

Wulff saw her reaction and smiled. Placing one hand lightly on her shoulder, he said, "Don't worry, Brittany. I'm just a lot of talk. My name may be Wulff, but I don't go around biting pretty girls. Maybe a nibble now and then."

A confusing mixture of emotions swirled through her at the touch of his hand on her shoulder, so non-threatening, and yet incredibly sensuous.

Brittany wanted to push his hand away, but at the same moment she longed to reach out and touch his whiskered cheek, just there, where it twitched with a suggestive grin.

In the end she did neither, but stood, and in a voice that trembled slightly, said, "I'd better leave now."

She had to get away from him. She couldn't think with him so near, touching her, looking at her with those penetrating blue eyes of his. She had to be alone, alone to think things through.

His hand trailed from her shoulder down her arm and grasped her fingers.

"You don't have to go," he said gently, releasing her hand. "I promise to behave myself. Stick around and I'll take you up in the light. After all, that's what you rode all the way up here for. Isn't it?"

She avoided his eyes. "Yes, but I think I woke you. You probably want to go back to bed."

"Not really. I'd have been up hours ago, but I keep watch through the night when there's a storm. And last night's was a pretty good one, as you know."

"Well, I spent the night on Andros Island and came over just this morning. But it rained pretty hard there, too."

"I thought you said that you came here from Nassau," he said.

"Yes, I did. I mean, I was in Nassau before."

"I see..." he said. She prayed that he didn't. "Well, Nurse Brittany, have a seat over there on the sofa and give me a few minutes to wash my face and comb my hair. Then I'll show you what it's like up where the seabirds fly.''

Chapter Two

Nestled into the cushions of Wulff's old but comfortable sofa, Brittany looked around the main room of the keeper's house. She had been so intent on the man himself that she had taken little notice of her surroundings.

The walls were the same natural gray stone as the outside of the building. Here and there a hook had been driven into the mortar to hold a painting of a clipper ship in full sail or a scene of tropical island beauty.

On the dark mahogany mantel of the stone fireplace sat a model of a schooner, captured forever inside a large, pale green bottle.

A strong solid sense of masculinity pervaded the room's furnishings, which were mostly heavy pieces of carved teak. Like the house, the furniture looked as though it had always been there and always would be.

Bits of brass gleamed in every corner—an antique diver's helmet, a ship's bell, a sextant and other nautical equipment.

The entire room glistened with not a spot of dust or dirt anywhere. Yet, there was a cosy, lived-in air about Wulff's home. As Brittany relaxed and felt her guard begin to drop, she reminded herself that this had been Captain Jonathan Wulff's house, too. Aren Wulff was his great-grandson, and she must never allow herself to forget that fact.

In front of the sofa an old pine chest with brass corners and fittings served as a coffee table. On the chest lay a thick leather-bound book that looked like a photo album. She was starting to reach for it when Wulff walked into the room.

His dark hair had been dampened and combed into a sleek style that she could tell wouldn't last long. Already, tiny curls had escaped around his ears and over his forehead.

His cheeks were slightly flushed from the razor's edge. The spicy scent of his after-shave drifted across the room to tickle her nose.

He had changed into a light cotton shirt that was the same pastel shade of blue as his eyes.

Brittany wondered if he realized how attractive he looked in that color and if he had chosen the shirt for that reason. She decided that he probably hadn't. She hadn't detected even the slightest streak of vanity in Aren Wulff.

He chose a banana from a bowl on the table. "Would you like something to eat? Or something else to drink? I have some fruit juice and maybe a soft drink in the kitchen."

Although the butterflies in her stomach had settled down a bit during his absence, Brittany still didn't think that she had any extra room for food or drink. "No, thank you. I've eaten. But you go ahead and have breakfast or lunch, or whatever you have when you first get up."

"I just did," he said, finishing the banana. "Come along, girl. Let's see if the pelicans are flying today."

He led her through a small kitchen, stopping along the way to toss the banana peel into a spotless garbage can. Then he reached inside a cupboard and took out a glass jar containing what appeared to be stale bread crusts.

"I have to feed Harvey, or he'll get peeved and buzz bomb the light," he explained.

"I see..." she muttered, nodding her head. "I'm so glad you explained that to me."

"No problem," he replied as he guided her out the back door and up a short flight of narrow steps that were cut into the stone. "If you have any questions, be sure to ask."

The stairs led them to the base of the lighthouse, which towered over their heads at least fifty feet. Unlike the irregular stones that comprised the house walls, the tower was constructed of uniformly shaped rectangular blocks. The mortared stones fit tightly together, creating a smooth, unblemished surface.

Brittany squinted at the eye-straining brilliance of the tower, which gleamed stark white in the afternoon sun.

"You must have to paint it often to keep it that white," she commented, blinking her eyes against the glare.

"Yes, we do. The salt sea air is pretty hard on it. It's about time to do it again."

She craned her neck backward, looking up to the top of the tower. "That's a long way up. It must be a tough job."

"It sure is," he said with a chuckle. "That's why we light keepers have to be tall."

Cocking her head sidewise, she gave him an exasperated grin.

"Okay," he said with a mock sigh as he opened a heavy metal door at the base of the tower. "I confess, I have to use a long paintbrush and stand on my toes. Otherwise I'd never make it."

"Thank you for clearing up that matter as well," she retorted. "I'm learning so much today."

In a small lean-to built against the tower, Brittany spotted a number of engines that she couldn't identify as belonging to lawn mowers, motorboats or anything else familiar.

"And I suppose that you'd be equally informative if I asked you what that is." She pointed to the largest engine.

"That's the generator. It provides power for the light and the house."

"How does it work?"

"It makes electricity."

Brittany groaned and shook her head. "Right. Thanks. I always wondered about that."

"So, now you know. After you—"

Brittany passed through the door and found herself standing at the bottom of a huge, white cylinder. In the center of the tower a narrow cast-iron staircase spiraled upward and disappeared into a hole at the top of the room. She cast a furtive glance at the heavy muscles in Wulff's legs. No wonder, with that many stairs to climb every day.

"How many steps are there?" she asked.

"Too many when you've got the flu, or when you're in your cups," he replied dryly, pointing to the staircase.

Brittany sighed and swept past him. Gripping the iron railing, she started up the narrow, twisting stairs with Wulff following several steps behind.

She stopped abruptly and turned to speak, causing him to nearly collide with her. "I hope you aren't charging much for this educationally enriching tour," she said.

Two steps below her, his eyes were level with her full, firm breasts. He openly appreciated the view for a couple of seconds, then lifted his gaze to hers. "You get what you pay for, girl, and I understood that you didn't want to spend very much." A suggestive smirk played upon his lips.

"I'd call that sexual harassment, wouldn't you?" she asked pointedly.

Wulff shrugged and then nodded thoughtfully. "I'd say it's pretty darned close."

Brittany turned on her heel and continued up the steps, trying to ignore his laughter as it echoed around her.

As she neared the top, she had the uncomfortable feeling that he was taking full advantage of the close, unobstructed view of her legs and rear end. Her indignation rose; she could practically feel the warmth of his eyes on her.

Then she remembered how pleasant it had been following him through the kitchen and out of the house, and how snugly his jeans fit his trim waist and hips. She had to admit that, given the chance, she would gladly follow Aren Wulff...anywhere...anytime.

Brittany tried to push the traitorous thought from her mind. After all, she wasn't on Wolf Island to appreciate the man's physique, no matter how nice it might be. She had important business to attend to.

Climbing the last few steps of the staircase, she passed through the hole at the top, out of the gloom and into the brilliance of the lantern chamber.

She stared in wonder at the center of the room where the lamp, shaped like a giant beehive made of mirrors and prisms, cast sparkling bits of rainbow color about the chamber.

The giant lantern, the heart of Wolf Light, slept peacefully through the daylight hours, patiently waiting for its night shift duty.

Brittany lifted her finger to touch one of its glistening, mirrored panels, but withdrew her hand when she saw that not a single fingerprint or spot of dust marred its polished surface. The lens looked more like an exquisite, modern sculpture than a functional piece of machinery.

Realizing that she had been holding her breath, Brittany released it in a long, soft sigh. "It's fantastic," she murmured.

She looked up and saw Wulff's intent gaze upon her. The mocking smirk had left his face and his eyes shone with pride and pleasure at her genuine interest in the lamp.

"Would you like to see how it works?" he asked quietly.

"Yes, I really would."

Wulff set the jar of bread crusts on the floor beside the staircase. Then he turned back to the lantern and carefully opened one side of the fragile dome.

"When my great-grandfather first lit this light-house, all he had was a primitive candelabra and a saucer-shaped reflector that smoked up continually and needed constant cleaning.

"When he died, my grandfather became keeper of the light. He replaced the old reflector with this Fresnel lens."

"Fresnel?"

"Yes. It's named after Augustin Fresnel, the man who invented it. The lens is a system of mirrors and glass that captures the light rays that are given off by a source inside the lamp, here."

He placed his hand on her back and drew her nearer to the lens. "And then it concentrates the light into a single horizontal beam."

Brittany tried to concentrate on his explanation, but it was difficult with his big hand splayed across her back and the crisp scent of his after-shave wafting about her.

Wulff opened the panel wider and with a gentle pressure on her back pulled her even closer to the lamp . . . and himself.

"Here, look inside. See the bulb? My father replaced the second source of light, a kerosene lamp, with an incandescent bulb. It was much brighter than the lamp, and it made life for the keeper a lot easier without all those smoky chimneys to clean and the wicks that continually needed trimming."

"Sounds like Wolf Light has advanced with the times," Brittany remarked appreciatively.

"We've all tried to leave our mark, so to speak. I've automated several of the systems. The light comes on and goes off by itself, and I replaced the old brass bell with a foghorn."

"Where is it?" Brittany asked, looking around the chamber.

"It's mounted on the boat house down by the beach. I wanted it as far away from the house and tower as possible. When that damn thing sounds, it makes your teeth rattle if you're near it."

His hand moved across her back to her shoulder and drifted down her arm to close firmly over her elbow. She was relieved that he stopped there. If his hand had traveled on down to her wrist he surely would have felt the erratic pulse that throbbed there. He led her away from the lens to the windows that surrounded the chamber.

"There's the boat house down there," he said.

Brittany looked down to where he was pointing and caught her breath. Through the glass she could see, far below her, the tiny white building and its dock.

But more than that, she saw the lush, emerald-green island spread at her feet and the sparkling turquoise sea, stretching into the distant horizon.

The water was so incredibly clear that she could see the reefs, blue holes, rocks and wreckage that littered the ocean floor. In the distance other green islands and hundreds of tiny cays poked their heads above the crystalline waters.

"Oh, my God," she whispered reverently. "This is magnificent."

"Come on." He guided her toward a glass door with one hand on her back. "It's even better from outside."

They passed through the narrow doorway and walked out onto an iron balcony that circled the lantern room. Brittany grasped the railing and breathed in the smell of sea air mixed with the delicate scent of the island's flowers.

She paused, savoring the sensuality of the moment. The tropical sun warmed her upturned face, as a velvet breeze caressed her skin and lingered in her hair, blowing it gently back over her shoulders.

Overhead, white seabirds dipped and dived through the cloudless blue sky, screeching their cacophonies to the waves that crashed onto the rocks in the cove below.

The cove. Wolf Cove. Brittany felt the peaceful tranquillity ebb as she looked down at the merciless rocks that devoured ships and their crews. Good men, with loved ones who waited and watched in vain for their men to return.

A silent rage welled up inside her. How could anyone be so heartless as to lure men to the teeth of this wolf to be eaten alive?

Moon cursers . . . devils who cursed the light of the moon and waited for dark, moonless nights to work their evil. Surely there was no greater wickedness that any man could do but to light a false fire and condemn his fellow man to a terrible, watery grave.

Yes, Brittany decided, there was one greater evil, one who was even more despicable than the moon curser. He was the man to whom had been entrusted the keeping of the lifesaving lamp. The man who, for a share of the moon curser's booty, would extinguish that light and betray his sacred trust.

Brittany thought of the pale blue eyes of Captain Jonathan Wulff. She looked up into those same eyes set in the face of his descendant, Aren Wulff. He stood, watching her with a touch of confusion on his handsome features.

"What is it?" he asked softly.

"What do you mean?"

He glanced down at the cove and then back at her. "You know what I mean. What is that cove to you?"

She tried to swallow, but her mouth was too dry. "Ah, Jesse told me that a lot of people died when they shipwrecked on those rocks."

"That's true," he replied thoughtfully. "But a lot of people were rescued when they wrecked down there, too. That's why we keep watch through the night when there's a storm—so that we can go out after them."

"Does that happen very often?" she asked.

"Often enough. Wolf Light was built as the result of a rescue. My great-grandfather saved the Grand Duke of Fryeburg when his ship ran aground here in 1855. The duke was so grateful that he granted Captain Jonathan a request, anything he wanted.

"He asked that the duke have a lighthouse built here on the rock so that it would warn ships away from the cove. The nobleman agreed and the building of the light was started a year later. It took three years and the duke's best builders to get the job done. But on September 4th, 1859, Captain Jonathan lit the lamp for the first time. Since then there have been wrecks from time to time, but not nearly as many as before."

Brittany stepped away from the railing and walked slowly around the balcony, digesting what she had heard. Wulff certainly painted a picture of Captain Jonathan that was very different from the image she had formed of the man.

"Have you ever had to go out after anyone?" she asked over her shoulder.

"Sure," he said, following closely behind her. "There's always some inexperienced yachtsman from the mainland down here on vacation who ignores the craft warnings and has to be bailed out of the brink. Or some drug runner risks his neck trying to get his contraband through no matter what the weather's like.

"Then, occasionally, one of the natives goes over to Andros for a bit of partying and finds it difficult to navigate through the fog with a rum-soaked brain.

"We go out after them, help them off their crafts or fish them out of the water. Then we bring them up to the house and dry them out. The next morning we give them a ride somewhere or help them get their boat off the rocks, if there's anything left, that is."

"Sounds like dangerous work."

A mirthless smile bowed his lips. "It can be." He stared down at the jagged, gray rocks of the cove and sighed heavily. "My parents died down there, trying to rescue a family that had run onto the rocks. The family survived...."

His voice trailed away, and for the first time his eyes wouldn't meet hers.

"I'm—I'm sorry," she stammered, embarrassed to have uncovered a painful memory.

Watching his hand tighten on the railing, she resisted the impulse to cover it with her own. She felt an instant kinship with him and his loss. "How old were you when it happened?"

"Fifteen," he replied shortly.

"My mother died when I was sixteen," she volunteered. "I know how hard it is to lose your parents when you're that young. Why were they both out there?"

"When a boat's in trouble, everybody goes out after them: the keeper, his wife and family, his assistant. That's just part of the job. I'd have been out there, too, but I was staying with my aunt in Miami at the time. My folks had sent me there to get an education since there aren't any schools on the island. I lived with my aunt until I graduated from college. Then I came back to Wolf Rock to keep the light. You know, family tradition and all that.''

Brittany studied his rugged face that glowed with the gold of the afternoon sun. Pride and satisfaction were etched in every tanned line of his countenance. There was almost an arrogance about the man. Yet Brittany detected no traces of egotism or selfishness.

She felt a tightening in her chest when she thought of Aren Wulff's pride in his ancestry. He had a heritage full of adventure, heroism, ultimate sacrifice and Captain Jonathan Wulff. She wondered what he would say when she told him that she knew about his heroic forefather.

For some reason she couldn't bear to think of that, so she pushed it to the back of her mind where it lay as heavy as a millstone.

"This lighthouse and your family tradition—they mean a lot to you, don't they?'' she asked quietly.

"Yes, I guess so. It's a good life, keeping Wolf Light. A bit lonely at times, but a worthwhile, challenging way to live. I like it. And how about you, Nurse Brittany, do you like your life?''

Brittany stared into the distance where the powder-blue of the sky met the turquoise of the sea. But instead of the tranquil scene before her, her mind's eye saw the bustling corridors of the general hospital where, until two weeks before, she had spent her days and a large part of her nights.

"I love being a nurse. I can't imagine doing anything else. It's what I've wanted to do since I was five years old. I like being able to help people and knowing that I've been instrumental in their healing. Of course, sometimes all you can do is hold their hand and offer whatever comfort you can. Yes, I really like nursing.''

His eyes searched her face, reaching into her thoughts. "But," he urged.

"But I hate the hospital where I work. It's a giant machine where patients are processed in one end and out the other. We're constantly understaffed, and there's no time for the extra attention that makes all the difference to the patients. The pace is so hectic. It's not what I had in mind when I decided to become a nurse."

Wulff watched her, fascinated by the ever-changing kaleidoscope of emotions on her pretty face; the passion when she spoke of her work, the frustration when she mentioned the hospital's frantic schedule.

He could imagine her there, competently dealing with a life-threatening crisis or taking the time to caress a fevered brow with that incredibly soft hand of hers.

"I'll bet you're a damn good nurse," he said. "In fact, I'd even bet that you've got great bedside manners."

He gave her a suggestive glance that caused her to giggle and turn that delicate shade of pink that he found positively irresistible.

"So, have you ever considered—" His question was interrupted by a shrill cry. A flapping brown missile careened over their heads, nearly striking them both.

"What the heck?" Brittany cried as she threw her arms around her head for protection.

Wulff laughed and strode briskly back to the door. "That's Harvey, our resident pelican. He's letting me know in his own tactful way that I haven't fed him today."

Brittany followed closely behind Wulff, not wanting to be left alone with an indignant, quarrelsome fowl. She trailed him back into the lantern chamber, where he retrieved the jar of bread crusts from the floor.

"A pelican who eats bread?" she asked.

"I soak it with fish oil first. I'm sure he'd prefer a nice swordfish fillet, but beggars can't be choosy," he said, grinning at her.

Staying safely inside the light room, she watched through the glass as Wulff returned to the balcony and dumped the crusts onto a small, square platform that was affixed to the railing.

Harvey, mollified by the sight of food, perched on the square and began to devour the bread.

Wulff watched him from several feet away, muttering tender obscenities to his feathered friend. A moment later he returned to the lantern chamber and his astonished guest.

"You've actually made a pet of that bird," she remarked incredulously.

"Well, he won't fetch my slippers or bark at intruders, but yes, I guess he's a pet of sorts. He certainly lets me know if I forget to feed him. Sometimes I think he's going to crash right through the glass and grab me by the collar. He's an assertive fellow. I guess that's why I like him."

Brittany watched as the bird greedily consumed the keeper's provisions. "I can see why he likes you," she said.

"Oh, I wouldn't say that he likes me. He just knows how to effectively intimidate me. We have a working agreement: I feed him; he doesn't bomb my light."

"Do you always succumb so easily to blackmail?"

"Only when the extortionist is as charming as Harvey. Feel free to blackmail me any time, Nurse Brittany. I promise to submit."

The very thought of Aren Wulff succumbing to her charms sent still another warm flush over Brittany's cheeks. God, how she wished that she didn't blush so easily. She looked up into his laughing, blue eyes, and he always seemed to notice.

"I'll keep that in mind," she sputtered nervously.

Glancing around the room, she sought some way to change the subject. "Do you have to stay up here every night to tend the lens?" she asked.

"Not every night. It's a very reliable system. I usually come up to check it once around midnight. And if the weather's bad, fog or rain, I stay all night, mainly to watch for wrecks."

"Don't you ever long for a full night's sleep with no interruptions or a night off?"

"Sure. Everybody has to get away once in a while. Sometimes I have my assistant take care of the light for the evening. But I really don't mind the nights. When I can't sleep, I come here and look at the moonlight shining on the water. It's so beautiful and peaceful that I relax enough to return to bed and get a good night's sleep."

Brittany wondered what would keep this confident, self-assured man awake. Then she remembered his reference to the dreams he had put aside. Perhaps those fantasies reasserted themselves during the midnight hour.

"It must be beautiful up here at night," she said.

Wulff turned toward her, his eyes memorizing every delicate feature of her face. "Absolutely gorgeous," he murmured.

"Tell you what, Nurse Brittany, I've got some things to do this afternoon before Jesse comes by for his reading lesson. But why don't you come back up to the point this evening about sundown? I'll make some dinner for us, and you can admire the view by moonlight."

His eyes swept over her again. "That way we'll both have something lovely to look at this evening."

Brittany hesitated, struggling with her mixed emotions. She was delighted to have another invitation to the light. After all, this was why she had come to the island, to become friends with Wulff and win his confidence.

So far, her mission had succeeded. She was sure that he liked her and was attracted to her. In fact, their meeting had gone much better than she had even dared to hope.

Yet, she was afraid of this man. It wasn't his tremendous size that frightened her or his rugged masculinity. She sensed that beneath his rough exterior lay the heart of a gentle giant.

She had seen the affection that he had shown for a lonely, little boy and a raucous pelican. She had felt his tender side when he had carefully bandaged her hand.

What frightened Brittany was her own response to Aren Wulff. When she had first arrived on the island, her greatest fear had been that she would reveal her hostility toward this descendant of Captain Jonathan Wulff. And yet, one look into his eyes and she felt all of her anger and prejudice floating away on a sea of acceptance—more than mere acceptance, if she were honest.

Brittany hadn't counted on the light keeper's good humor, his disarming smile or the raw masculinity that emanated from him, warming and exciting her whenever he touched her or even came near.

Did she dare trust herself to be alone with him in the moonlight at the top of the light? Something inside her whispered that if he decided to "take a nibble" as he had phrased it, she would never have the strength or even the will to resist.

"I'd like that very much," she found herself saying.

"Good. Have you ever eaten conch chowder?"

"No, I haven't. Do I want to?" she asked suspiciously.

"Sure, it's great stuff. A staple around here. It'll be ready about seven, if that fits into your heavy itinerary."

"I'll have to cancel tea with the queen. I hope she understands."

"She will if you tell her I'm making conch chowder. It's one of her favorites."

Brittany smiled and started toward the staircase. "I'll be sure to give her your regards."

"You do that. Can you find your own way down? I have some work to do up here, now that you've brought me the fuses."

"Sure, no problem. Thank you for the personally guided tour, Mr. Wulff," she tossed over her shoulder as she began her descent.

"Hey, you forgot to pay me," he called after her. "That's okay, I'll collect my fee later... with interest."

* * *

Picking her way carefully down the steep, rocky stairway and through the gate, Brittany finally arrived at the spot where she had left Debra's bicycle by the side of the road.

She had the distinct feeling that she was being watched. Glancing up at the tower, she thought she saw a movement near the glass. On impulse she waved and felt a disturbingly intense surge of pleasure when she saw a giant hand wave back.

"Darn him," she muttered as she pedaled down the hill.

Aren Wulff watched her until she disappeared around the curve at the bottom of the point.

Why did she have to have all that beautiful blond hair? he asked himself. Why hadn't she come along twenty years ago when he was still naive enough to believe in love at first sight? And why did she have to be his type?

Well, actually she wasn't quite his type, just almost. He preferred his women a little older with a bit more spark, a bit more fire.

Yet, he could swear that there was a strength of spirit in that girl, a solidity that you could depend on. But someone or something had temporarily weakened her, knocked the wind out of her sails.

He recalled the pain that had shown in those strange, golden eyes of hers when she thought that he wasn't watching. She had been hurt—badly—recently.

Aren Wulff decided that there was more to pretty Nurse Brittany than met the eye at first glance.

What was she hiding? And why, why did she look so familiar? He would figure it out sooner or later. He always did.

Chapter Three

An hour after making arrangements with Debra's grandmother, Brittany stood surveying the one-room cabin that was to be her home for the next few weeks.

Sparsely furnished, the room contained only a small wrought iron daybed and a card table with two rickety folding chairs. On the table sat a hurricane lamp, the room's only light, and a box of wooden matches. A door in the back wall led to a miniature bathroom.

A bit primitive, she thought as she checked the rusty plumbing, but at least it works.

She jumped as the faucet sputtered and spewed amber water on her already hopelessly soiled shorts.

"Well, it's not the Ritz," she muttered under her breath. "But like Debra said, it's clean. Besides, it's not like I'm here on vacation."

She walked back into the main room and laid her one suitcase on the bed. After changing her splattered clothes for lavender slacks and a white gauze blouse, she abandoned the suitcase where it lay. Unpacking could wait.

Five short paces took her across the tiny room to the northern window on the front of the house. Pushing aside the threadbare, sun-faded curtains, she could see a stretch of gloriously white beach and ocean water so crystal clear that she could scarcely tell where the water ended and the beach began.

In the distance, snowy white triangles sailed across the misty blue of the sea, and an occasional cabin cruiser left its foaming wake on the water's gently rolling surface.

Brittany closed her eyes and allowed the serenity of the ocean to seep into her troubled, aching soul, warming and healing all that it touched.

She breathed a sigh of contentment, the first in months, and opened her eyes. Maybe coming to Wolf Island would be good for her after all, more than an obligation that she had to fulfill.

Reluctantly she turned away from the view and crossed the room to the window at the back of the house. From this southern exposure she could see the small town, the only town, on Wolf Island.

About two hundred people lived in the tiny village of pastel limestone cottages. Children romped with their dogs in the streets while their elders carried baskets laden with fish and sponges gathered from the sea.

A certain respect, even a bit of envy, stirred inside Brittany as she watched them casually perform their duties and as she compared their peaceful lives with hers at the hospital.

As natural and unaffected as the shifting tides, the islanders lived without the luxuries of wealthier societies. And yet, as she watched them, Brittany had the impression that their simple lives were infinitely richer.

She sighed and crossed to the remaining window in the western wall of the cottage. Her breath caught when she saw the dazzling picture framed by the sill.

Rising high above the lush, tropical greenery that covered the island was Wolf Rock. Gray-blue in the late afternoon light, it jutted sharply into the golden, Caribbean sky. And crowning the rock was Wolf Lighthouse.

Her brother, Michael, had told her that the lighthouse was interesting, even fascinating. But he had never told her that it was breathtakingly beautiful, that it glowed like a precious jewel atop the emerald velvet of the island.

But then, Michael had neglected to tell her that his friend, the light keeper, had sparkling blue eyes, or that he could bandage a woman's hand with a tenderness that made her ache to lay her head against his chest and feel his strong muscular arms steal around her.

Yes, there was a lot that Michael hadn't told her about Aren Wulff.

Brittany closed her eyes and allowed the thoughts of Michael to come, filling her with a bittersweet flood of emotions. She felt much closer to him here on the island than she had back in Orlando. It was as though a remnant of his spirit was here, as if he had left something of himself behind in this place and she could feel him nearby.

Opening her eyes, she looked up again at the lighthouse.

"I'm finally here, Michael," she whispered. "I'm here and I'm not leaving until I finish what you started.

I promise that I'll make your dream come true, whatever it costs.''

That evening the long ride up to Wolf Light was less taxing than it had been earlier in the day. This time Brittany avoided all of the mud puddles and had no unexpected encounters with speckled puppies and red-haired boys.

As she neared the top of the point, Brittany could see the endless expanse of water, stained vermilion by the setting sun.

Her eyes searched the smooth surface as she wondered where it had happened.

Part of her didn't want to know, didn't want to look at the spot of ocean where her brother had died. But another stronger part of her had to see the place with her own eyes, and in seeing, share something of her brother's death.

She wanted to ask Wulff about it, but she knew that she couldn't. One mention of Michael and he would know who she was and why she had come to the island. Then he would turn her away, just as he had turned Michael away.

He had made it clear that morning that he still felt the same way about treasure seekers and fortune hunters. If he had refused to help Michael, his best friend, what made her think he would help her? Especially since she had already attempted to deceive him.

Brittany had the strong impression that the light keeper would not take kindly to being lied to. She also had the feeling that he would be a dangerous man to cross. Anger was definitely not a passion that she wanted to stir in Aren Wulff.

As she left the bicycle beside the gate, she looked up at the sign of the wolf's head above her.

Brittany shuddered. She wasn't sure why. Was it because she recalled the tattoo on the light keeper's muscular arm? Or was it because she remembered what the wolf's head symbolized?

Either way, she cautioned herself to be extremely careful tonight.

Aren Wulff's door stood ajar, and as Brittany stepped up onto the porch, she could hear the drone of his deep voice floating out to her from the living room. She quietly walked to the door and peeked inside.

Wulff and Jesse sat close together on the old sofa, their heads bent over a book. The golden light from a lamp in the corner set Wulff's dark hair and Jesse's flaming locks afire with glittering highlights of copper and gold.

Jesse was curled against his friend's brawny arm. His tiny feet, encased in ragged sneakers, were propped on the old chest beside Wulff's huge deck shoes.

In rich, deep tones the light keeper's voice recited the words of Robert Louis Stevenson's *Treasure Island*. And like the generations of boys who had listened before him, Jesse hung breathlessly on every syllable.

Brittany listened for several minutes, unwilling to break the spell that Wulff was weaving for his young companion.

Then she heard him say, "Well, that's the end of that chapter. What do you think, mate?"

Jesse beamed. "I'm glad Jim got that old Mr. Hands. Serves him right. I'll bet he ain't dead, though. He just fell in the water, that's all."

"Well, let me see. . . ." Wulff lifted the book out of Jesse's view and skimmed the next few pages. "Oh, no," he said with a gasp, "this is really awful, poor Jim."

"What . . . what is it?" Jesse asked breathlessly.

"I can't tell you. It's too bad. In fact, I don't think I'd better read this chapter to you tomorrow. We'll skip over this part. It's not fit for little boys to hear."

"Oh, you!" Jesse socked Wulff's massive arm with his puny fist. "You always say that."

"Oww!" Wulff rubbed the spot on his biceps. "You big bully, why don't you pick on somebody your own size."

"'Cause it's more fun to pick on you!" In a split second Jesse had pounced on the keeper and pulled him onto the floor in front of the sofa.

With ear-splitting squeals of delight, Jesse poured all of the energy of a feisty seven-year-old into a valiant attempt to subdue his giant opponent.

Wulff absorbed the feeble blows for several minutes.

"So, you wanna play rough, huh," he rumbled. "Okay, you asked for it. Now you're gonna get it good."

With one swift movement he had the boy pinned to the floor. He kneeled over him, growling ominously, "Well, mates, we've got the dirty little bilge rat now. What shall we do with him?"

Jesse wriggled beneath Wulff and screamed, "Release him, let him go."

"Nay, never. He's dirty, traitorous scum, he is. Shall we hang him from the yardarm?" Wulff inquired of his invisible shipmates.

"Nay! Nay!" screamed Jesse at the top of his lungs.

"Aye, you're right. Hanging's too good for the bloody bugger. Let's make 'im walk the plank."

"Nay! Nay!" Jesse protested again.

"Well, why not?" Wulff demanded. "Sounds good to me."

"'Cause...'cause the plank broke the last time we used it. Remember? That big, fat pirate broke it clean off, just before the sharks got 'im."

"Aye, that's right, it slipped me mind. Well, I guess we'll just have to pitch him overboard, send him down to Davy Jones's locker. Aye, that's what we'll do."

"Nay, have mercy!" Jesse screamed as Wulff picked him up and tossed him, kicking and yelling, over his broad shoulder.

Wulff bore his struggling burden to the door where he grabbed the boy by his hands and feet.

"Here he goes, mates," he cried, opening the door the rest of the way with his foot.

He had lifted the boy as though to throw him out the door when he spotted Brittany standing there with her mouth hanging open.

"Wait, hold everything," Wulff exclaimed, suspending Jesse in midair. "What have we here? A winsome wench right on our very deck."

He lowered Jesse and stood him on his feet. "Well, we can't throw a man overboard in front of a lady, now can we?"

"Nay, never in front of a lady," Jesse agreed heartily.

"Well, I guess you've been granted a reprieve for today, but you won't be so lucky the next time you fall into our clutches, you bloody traitor. Be off with you. If you don't reach port by sundown, your granny will have both our hides."

Brittany and Wulff laughed as they watched the boy scurry down the steps and through the gate.

"And what fate would he have suffered if I hadn't arrived in the nick of time?" Brittany asked as he ushered her inside.

"We would have pitched the lad overboard, of course." Wulff ran his fingers through his mussed hair and tucked his shirttail back into his jeans.

"Don't look so shocked, Nurse Brittany. I always make sure he lands on his feet. Getting thrown overboard is the high point of Jesse's reading lesson. He counts on it."

"Then I hope that he wasn't too disappointed in his reprieve today."

"Oh, that's okay. I'll make it up to him tomorrow. I'll run 'im through with my sword before I throw him to the sharks."

"Mmm, what smells so good?" Brittany asked, breathing in the spicy aroma that filled the house.

"That, my dear, is the infamous Wolf Light chowder. I think it's about ready, if you're hungry."

"I wasn't, but after smelling that, I'm starved."

"Good, step this way." He led her to the kitchen where the source of the aroma bubbled in a large clay pot on the stove.

"I was thinking about a picnic instead of a formal dinner. Does that suit your fancy?" he asked as he ladled the thick red stew into a small crock.

"Sounds great. May I help?"

"Sure, look in the refrigerator and get that plate of fruit."

She opened the small door and found a platter that brimmed with chunks of pineapple, mango and papaya.

"This looks great," she said, "but I'm afraid you went to a lot of unnecessary trouble. Do you enjoy cooking?"

"Not particularly. But I love to eat good food. It's my second favorite sensual pastime," he replied smoothly.

His eyes swept over her, burning through the front of her thin gauze blouse. She was mortified to feel her breasts responding shamelessly to the heat of his gaze. Maybe he wouldn't notice— He noticed. He grinned and glanced away.

"I had to learn how to cook," he continued. "You can't exactly send out for pizza or fried chicken on this island, you know.

"Here." He handed her a loaf of bread wrapped in a blue napkin. "If you can take that, too, I think we can make it in one trip."

"Where are we going? The beach?" she asked.

"We'll do that some time if you like," he replied, taking the handle of the pot in one hand and a small picnic basket in the other. "This evening we'll dine at the top of the island. The view's magnificent and to-night—" his eyes swept her length from head to toe "—tonight the scenery is exquisite."

"Inside or out?" Brittany asked when they had climbed the last step and entered the lantern chamber.

"Outside, of course. You want to be able to share your dinner with Harvey, don't you?"

She gave him a horrified look. "Not really. He didn't exactly make a good first impression on me this afternoon."

"Don't worry. I was just kidding. He's probably out trying to find himself some bit of cuddlesome fluff to bed down with for the night. Smart fellow, Harvey."

"And is that what you're doing, Mr. Wulff, with all of your sexual innuendos?"

"What's that?" he asked, opening the door to the balcony.

"You know what. Trying to find a bit of cuddlesome fluff."

"Why, Nurse Brittany, you do have a suspicious mind," he murmured as she passed close to him and out the door onto the balcony.

"Around here." He led her to the western side of the lighthouse, where the sun lay, a glowing half orb, upon the ocean.

The golden light tinted the entire scene with a warm Midas touch. The islands were a deep charcoal, the sky a delicate honey and the waters a vibrant amber.

Wulff laid the basket and pot of chowder on the fine iron mesh of the balcony floor and reached for the platter of fruit and bread.

"Have a seat right there, and I'll have this ready before you know it."

Brittany sat where he had indicated, leaning her back against the wall of the tower. The stones still held their heat from the day's sun. It warmed the stiff, tense muscles of her back, causing her to relax and realize how tired she was.

It seemed like another lifetime since she had hired the boat and sailed to Wolf Island. It had been a long day, and it wasn't over yet.

Wulff spread a blue batik-printed cloth. Upon it he placed two teak bowls, spoons, a dish of butter, two glasses and a bottle of opaque white juice.

"Mai-tai without the tai," he explained, pouring the drinks. "See, I remembered."

"Thank you," she said softly, as a fleeting trace of pain flashed in her golden eyes again.

Wulff studied her carefully, then lifted his glass to her. "To the lovely, mysterious Nurse Brittany. May we learn all of her deep, dark secrets."

"I—I don't think I can drink to that," she stammered.

"Okay, let's qualify it then. May we learn only those secrets that she decides to trust to us."

"Who's us?"

"Me."

She lifted her glass and returned his steady gaze. "Okay, and here's to you, Aren Wulff," she said as their glasses met. "And to a time when maybe secrets won't be necessary."

"May it be soon," he added before tasting the coconut-flavored concoction. Setting his glass aside, he handed her a bowl of chowder and a chunk from the loaf of bread.

Brittany raised a spoonful of the steaming broth to her lips and sipped. "Whoa! That's potent!" she exclaimed, fanning her tongue and reaching for her drink.

Wulff chuckled as he watched her attempt to extinguish the flames. "I call it spicy. That's the way I like it. I figured that you'd like it spicy, too."

"Oh, do I seem like the spicy type to you?"

He eyed her lips lasciviously. "Maybe. We'll see. You don't have to eat that if it's too much for you."

"It's delicious," she replied, choosing a bit of carrot from among the chunks of celery, carrots and conch that floated in the rich, tomato broth. "I just wasn't expecting it, that's all."

"Well, be prepared in the future, girl." His eyes sparkled wickedly. "I dish it up hot and spicy."

She shook her head in feigned disgust. "Aren't conceited now, are you?"

"Maybe a bit. But wait and see if you don't agree after you've sampled my...cooking."

Brittany choked on the bit of carrot. "Perhaps we'd better discuss something besides your cooking," she said when she caught her breath.

"Okay." Wulff slowly sipped his drink. "Jesse says that you've rented that little cabin of theirs on the beach."

"Yes, I did. It's small, but it suits my purpose."

"And what purpose is that?" he asked, studying the design on his glass.

"It's a place to live for a while."

He stared at her with his piercing blue gaze. "For how long?"

She squirmed against the stone wall. "Oh, a couple of weeks, maybe a bit more."

"So, is that how long you figure it'll take to get whatever it is that you want from me?"

Brittany set her glass down quickly so that he wouldn't see her hand tremble. She searched her mind for an answer, but couldn't think of anything to say.

"What's the matter? We can't seem to find a topic of conversation that you're comfortable with, can we?"

"I'm sorry," she replied sincerely.

"So am I. Why don't you trust me and tell me what this is all about?"

Brittany could feel her lower lip begin to quiver and cursed herself for her weakness. She had never been like this before, always on the verge of tears, at least, not before Michael's death. "It's not that easy."

"Obviously not," he replied thoughtfully. "Okay, you choose. What would you like to talk about?"

"Tell me about Wolf Cove," she said, biting into the soft brown bread.

"What would you like to know about it?"

"Whatever you'd like to tell me."

"Well, it's been there for a long time."

"That's good to know. Nobody trusts a fly-by-night cove."

Wulff laughed and continued, "Yes, well, years ago this not so trustworthy cove was a haven for moon cursers. On a dark night it looks like a nice, safe little harbor. You can't see the rocks until you're well into it, and by then it's too late. Plus, there are strong currents at the mouth of the cove that will suck you right in if you're not careful. Sometimes even if you are. Then there are the squalls, and the fog can get pretty heavy at times. All in all, it's a great place to set up shop, if you're a wrecker. Hey!" He reached over and grabbed her hand and the piece of bread that was in transit to her mouth. "You aren't going to eat your crusts, are you?"

"I was going to. Why?"

He gave her an exasperated grin. "You have to ask?"

She searched her mind for a moment. It wasn't easy to think with his hand clasping hers. Then a light came on in her head. "Harvey?"

"Of course." With his other hand he took the crust from her and piled it on the cloth next to his.

"Sorry, I don't know what came over me," she mumbled. He still hadn't released her hand. How was she going to finish eating? Not that she really cared. Her appetite had quickly waned at his touch.

"That's okay, this time. I won't tell him. Anyway, the wreckers had a great old time down there. They used the caves around the cove to hide their loot. It was a pretty good setup."

"Until the lighthouse was built?"

"Yes, and a lot of them were caught, taken to England and hanged. That's when the rest of them decided that they'd better relocate. I understand that they mostly worked on Andros after that, especially during the American Civil War. But for the most part they stayed away from Wolf Cove."

"Does it ever bother you—living in a place where there's been so much death and violence?"

He took a deep breath and slowly released her hand. "I was raised here. The place is a part of me and I guess I don't think about it. Besides, they say that the cove has its own means of dealing out justice."

"What do you mean?" she asked, tilting her bowl to retrieve the last drop of chowder.

"Well," he murmured in a conspiratorial tone, "there are these legends...."

His voice trailed away as he gathered up the dishes and packed them back into the basket. Then he moved closer to Brittany. With his back against the railing he faced her, his eyes twinkling with secret amusement.

"The old people on the island say that those who have died in the cove get their revenge on the wreckers who murdered them."

"How?" she asked skeptically.

"Well, have you ever heard of 'him of de hands'?"

"No, I'm afraid not."

"The natives believe that 'him of de hands' is a creature who lives in the blue holes of the sea and comes up every now and then to grab some hapless sailor and his boat. They also believe that the victims of Wolf Cove have a pact with 'him of de hands.' This rather unpleasant fellow uses fog, storms, currents, whatever he chooses to lure the wreckers who have murdered these people back into the cove. Then the victims reach up and grab the wreckers right out of their boats and pull them down into the black, swirling waters to their deaths."

"I see," she muttered, solemnly nodding her head. "And is this an authentic legend, Mr. Wulff, or are you making this up as you go?"

"Why, Nurse Brittany, you wound me to the quick. Certainly it's authentic. Ask Jesse's granny if you don't believe me."

"And does this phenomenon occur often?"

"Of course not." He leaned toward her and whispered ominously, "Only when the moon's full."

"Of course, silly me." Brittany toyed with the lace on the front of her blouse. "So, tell me, Mr. Wulff, do you believe this legend?"

"Certainly not. I don't believe in old wives' tales."

Wulff languidly stretched his long legs out before him. "But then, I stay out of the cove whenever possible if it's full moon."

"Why? You aren't a wrecker."

"No, but there's no point in taking chances."

"I think you're pulling my leg."

His eyes swept the length of her legs stretched beside his. Even through the fabric of her slacks, he could discern the well-rounded calves and shapely thighs that had captured his attention earlier.

"Now there's an appealing thought," he murmured, giving her a playful smile that caused her insides to turn to jelly.

She quickly looked away, afraid that he would read in her eyes how appealing the thought was to her, too.

"Sun's down," she commented awkwardly.

"Moon's up, stars out," he added. "Any more news bulletins?"

At that moment they heard the hum of a motor, and a rotating beam pierced the gathering darkness over their heads.

"Light's on," they exclaimed simultaneously.

As they laughed together Brittany felt a bond beginning to grow between them. It would be so easy to reach over and touch him.

"You have a lovely smile, Brittany." His voice was low and soothing. "You should smile more often."

"I used to," she answered, looking down at her hands, which lay folded in her lap.

"That's what I thought." He watched as her fingernail traced the edge of the bandage. "Do you want to tell me about it?"

Brittany looked up into his eyes, which shone with compassion. She had the feeling that Aren Wulff was the one person to whom she could pour out her heart. Michael had been his friend, too. He would know, if anyone could, how she felt, how much she missed her brother, his easy smile, his frequent laughter, his corny jokes.

For a moment she entertained the thought of laying her head on Wulff's broad chest, crying out her sorrow and sharing her loss with him.

Yes, she wanted to tell him all about it.

"I'd like to, very much," she said. "But I can't. Maybe some other time."

He sighed softly and looked disappointed. "Yes, maybe some other time."

Wulff reached across the short space between them and lightly trailed one rough finger along her cheek. He heard her sharp intake of breath and wondered at her reaction. He allowed himself to consider what she might do if he tried to kiss her.

He could tell that she was frightened. But her eyes were warm, warm and . . . pleading? What the hell did she want from him? Looking at her now, he would give her the world if she asked for it. But she didn't. She just sat there, watching him. Waiting.

He wound the end of her hair ribbon around his finger. "May I?" he asked, tugging at it gently.

Her lips silently framed the word, yes.

Wulff pulled at the bit of satin until it released a glimmering cascade of curls that tumbled over her shoulder and onto her breast.

He breathed a sigh of appreciation and lifted one golden strand, then let it slip slowly through his fingers.

"It is," he murmured, more to himself than to her.

"It is what?" she asked.

"Your hair, it's as soft as it looks, even softer."

His finger moved back to her cheek and gently stroked its silkiness.

At his touch, Brittany felt the well of emotions inside her heart brim nearly to overflowing.

She had been so alone the past two months and in need of comfort. There had been no one to console her and no one to show her tenderness. The one who had always done that was gone forever.

And now, here was a man whose genuine concern for her was etched as clearly as the tanned lines on his face.

She followed the bidding of her heart and held out her arms to him.

"Wulff, help me, please," she pleaded.

In a moment he had gathered her into his lap and was holding her, cradled against his chest.

"Of course I will, girl. I'll help you. But you have to let me know what you want from me. I don't understand."

Brittany looked up into his handsome face, only inches from hers. His warm breath fanned her cheek. She could feel the hard swell of the muscles in his arms, which were wrapped tightly about her waist. She watched as her own arms wound around his neck, her palm gliding over the tiny wisps of hair that curled over his shirt collar.

At that moment she knew exactly what she wanted from Aren Wulff. Lifting her lips toward his, she tangled her fingers in his thick, dark hair and pulled his head down to hers.

She thought that she saw a fleeting look of surprise in his eyes. A second later they closed and his mouth descended on hers.

At first he teased her, his lips grazing hers with light, feathery brushings. A series of tremors raced down her body to shake the epicenter of her femininity.

Then his mouth covered hers, warmer, fuller than she had even imagined. His arms tightened around her, pulling her to him until her soft breasts were pressed against the hardness of his chest. They both reveled in the contrast.

Deep within her the quake began and rippled through her body. Somewhere inside, a floodgate burst, filling her with uncontrollable emotions.

She clung to Wulff as though he were a lifeline. Her hands at the back of his head forced his mouth down on hers, harder and harder.

He responded with a moan deep in his throat and plunged his hot, moist tongue into the honeyed recesses of her mouth. She shivered with delight as she submitted to its insistent probings and answered with flicks of her own across his lower lip.

When Wulff felt her body shudder in his arms, his final thread of self-control snapped. Bending her backward in his arms, he laid her across his lap and leaned over her, his mouth never leaving hers.

His right hand slid up her back and burrowed its way through the golden mass of curls, becoming deliciously entangled in the silken strands.

She whimpered softly as again and again his tongue thrust between her parted lips, entering her, taking her, mating with her, as his body ached to do.

Wulff was taken aback by her urgent responses. Her arms circled his back and clutched him even tighter to her ample bosom. The kisses that she returned to him were nearly frantic with desire.

Never before had he held such a vibrant, passionate woman in his arms. He felt seared by the heat of her breasts as they crushed against him. Her mouth devoured his with a hunger that was even more ravenous than his own.

He longed to lose himself in her, to drown in her warmth, her fragrant softness. But something was wrong. He fought his way through the fog of desire, trying to understand what was happening.

Then he realized: he was hungry; but she was desperate.

Abruptly he ended the kiss. He pulled her up from his lap and held her at arm's length. "Wait. Hold on a minute," he said. "Give me a second to catch my breath."

Brittany said nothing, but waited, listening to the sounds of their labored breathing and feeling the trembling in the giant hands that held hers. What was wrong? Why had he pulled away?

"I'd decided that I wasn't going to do this. I really did," he said, his voice still husky from desire. "I was kidding around with you, girl. I wasn't really going to go for it."

"Why not?" she asked.

"Because I think you're vulnerable right now for some reason that you don't want to talk about, and I don't want to take advantage of you." He took a deep breath. "Besides, you're too young."

"Too young!" she exclaimed, snatching her hands away from his.

"Yes. Hell, I'm old enough to be your father."

"That's ridiculous. You couldn't possibly be my father." She stopped, thought for a moment and added, "Unless you got an awfully early start."

"How old are you?"

"Twenty-five."

He looked away, mentally calculating, then smiled as though recalling a pleasant memory.

"Yep, I could be your father...barely." He grinned impishly and added, "There's not much to do when you're a teenager on this island."

"Well, the point is that you're not my father, and I'd appreciate it if you'd stop calling me a girl. I'm a woman. If you're lucky, I might prove that to you someday."

She stopped, blushed at her own words and then continued. "And another thing, you don't have to worry about taking advantage of me. For your information, I don't allow people to take advantage of me."

Wulff stared at her, astonished by her outburst. So, there was fire in Nurse Brittany after all. A moment before it had blazed in her kisses, and now it smoldered in her eyes—those strange, golden eyes, like a cat's glowing in the dark.

Wulff's face grew hard and his eyes narrowed to slits. His hands encircled her wrists like steel manacles.

"What?" she asked. "Aren, what is it?"

"You come with me, girl," he growled, dragging her to her feet. "You've got some explaining to do."

Chapter Four

You're hurting my wrist," Brittany complained as Wulff dragged her through the kitchen and into the living room.

"Consider yourself lucky that it isn't your pretty little neck that's getting squeezed. Here, have a seat."

Unceremoniously he deposited her on the sofa and stood, glowering over her. Even in the warm golden light of the lamp his eyes glinted like cold steel. Brittany wondered how she had ever considered his gaze to be kind.

Wulff grabbed the leather album that lay on the chest and began flipping through its pages.

He quickly found what he was looking for. Removing a snapshot, he held it for a moment, studying first the photo and then her face.

With a flick of his wrist he tossed the picture into her lap.

She picked it up with fingers that still ached from his relentless grip. Brittany looked at the photo briefly before her vision began to blur with tears.

It was a picture of Wulff, smiling, holding a fishing pole in one hand. His other arm was draped across the shoulders of a much shorter blond man with a broad smile and laughing eyes.

And even though the picture was too small to reveal details, both Brittany and Wulff knew that the man's eyes were an unusual shade of gold, the color of topaz.

Brittany felt the breath leave her body in a single sob. Closing her eyes, she tried to blot the picture from her mind. It was the first time she had seen Michael's face since she had received word of his death.

She had carefully avoided seeing any photographs of him for fear that it would make her sense of loss even more acute. Yet, here he was, smiling at her with that lazy, disarming charm of his—a smile that she would never see again except in photographs.

Wulff's voice cut through her anguish. "I guess I should have thought to ask your last name. Or would you have lied about that, too, Susie?"

"I didn't lie about my name. It is Brittany."

Wulff snatched the photograph from her hand. "Come on, girl. Now would be a perfect time to cut the bull and start telling the truth for a change."

"I am telling you the truth. My name is Brittany Suzanne Davis. My brother was the only one who ever called me . . . that."

She couldn't bring herself to say the pet name she had complained about for years. She certainly wouldn't complain now. But Michael was gone and he would never call her that again.

Wulff lowered his bulk into an overstuffed chair across from her. His face was still as hard as flint and his eyes glittered with anger.

"So, let's see now," he muttered, folding his arms in front of him and settling back into the chair. "Why did you really come to Wolf Island? And why didn't you tell me who you are?"

"I didn't think you would exactly welcome me," she said, relieved that she could finally be honest with him.

"Why would you assume that I wouldn't welcome you? After all, you're the little sister of my best friend who just recently passed on. You should have known that I'd treat you right, for Michael's sake if nothing else."

Brittany rubbed her wrist; the feeling was beginning to return to her hand. Wulff watched her, some of the anger leaving his face.

"I'm sorry about your arm. But damn it, I don't like being lied to. In fact, it's about my least favorite thing in life."

"I'm sorry, Aren," she murmured. She looked directly into his eyes, trying to convey her sincerity. "Really, I hated lying, especially to you. It's just that this is so important, and I was afraid that you'd send me away."

"So, what is it that's so all-fired important to you?"

"I . . ." She fumbled for the right words.

"Now don't lie to me again. I can tell and it ticks me off."

"I won't. I promise I'll never lie to you again. I'm trying to think of the right words."

"Well, stop thinking and just say it. What do you want from me? Out with it. I'm getting tired of this."

She dropped all pretenses, took a deep breath and said, "I want you to help me find my great-grandfather Davis's cargo, the stuff that Michael was looking for when he died."

Wulff pounded his fist on the cushioned arm of the chair. "Bloody hell! I swear, this insanity must be hereditary. You're crazy. The whole lot of you are bloody crazy."

He rose from his chair and began pacing the floor in front of her. "Now I see. You're down here on a damned treasure hunt, after all. No wonder you wouldn't tell me what you wanted. You knew I'd boot you out on your shapely little rear if you did."

Brittany felt her temper rising along with the color in her cheeks. "Sure," she snapped, "after all, that's what you did to Michael, isn't it? You turned your back on him when he needed you. Maybe he'd be alive today if you'd been a friend to him and helped him."

Shaking with the intensity of her anger, she steadfastly returned Wulff's glare. She watched his jaw tighten and his face grow white with rage as he stared down at her.

"Don't you lay that on me, girl. Don't you dare. I tried to warn that brother of yours. I told him time and time again to get control of his damned greed. But would he listen to me? Hell, no. He died because he was looking for a fast buck, not because I turned my back on him."

Brittany rose to her feet, her fists clenched at her sides. "Don't you dare say anything like that about my brother. Michael was not greedy. He was a fine person, the best."

She felt the sobs that lay just below the surface begin to rise in her throat. "My brother took care of me when our mom died. He raised me and made a home for me. He was ambitious, sure. But he only wanted what he thought was his and his family's. Michael was a good person. He was."

Hot tears spilled down her cheeks. Brittany quickly brushed them away, unwilling to show any weakness to the man who stood before her, his hands shoved deep into his pockets, his brow furrowed in thought.

He sighed and studied the space of floor between them. "Look, Michael was a good man in many ways. I cared about him, too, you know. I'm glad that he was a fine brother to you. And if you want to remember him as a saint, I won't take that away from you.

"I'm sorry that he's dead. I'm sorry that wreckers killed your great-grandfather and stole his cargo. I'm sorry about it all. But what's done is done and we can't change the past. Forget it all, girl, and go on. Don't throw your life away like your brother did."

Suddenly, Brittany felt very tired, defeated. "You're not going to help me, are you?" she asked tearfully.

Wulff hesitated, lifted his hand as though to reach out to her, and then thrust it back into his pocket.

"Yes, I'm going to help you. Tonight I'm going to walk you back to that little cabin that you're staying in. And tomorrow morning I'm going to take you to Andros, where you can catch a plane back to Orlando. Believe me, that's the best thing that I can possibly do for you."

A dark cloud of depression settled over Brittany's soul, the darkest since Michael's death. She had failed him. It was the last thing she could do for her brother to repay him for all he had done for her. And she had failed.

She walked past Wulff and headed for the door, her head down and her shoulders slumped. She was tired, too tired even for anger.

"I'm sorry that I lied to you," she said, "and that I wasted your time."

He reached out and briefly touched her shoulder as she passed. "You weren't a waste of time, Nurse Brittany," he said softly. "I just wish that things had been different."

He took her hand and tucked it into the crook of his arm. "Come along, now. Get a good night's sleep and you'll feel better in the morning."

He opened the door and guided her through it. When they reached the porch, she pulled her hand away from him.

"I don't need you to walk me home," she said, descending the stairs.

Wulff followed her. "I don't mind."

"I do," she said simply and walked away, leaving him standing on the steps.

"But I'll worry about you, girl," he called after her.

"Don't," she called back. "I keep telling you, I'm not a girl. I'm a woman. And I'll be all right."

Brittany moaned and covered her eyes with her arm, shielding them from the bright sunlight that streamed through the dingy curtains.

Her head ached from crying half of the night, and the muscles in her legs complained bitterly about the exercise that she had subjected them to the day before.

When she had fallen into bed last night she had somehow thought that it was the end. Everything was over. She had forgotten that the sun would rise, and there would be yet another day to face.

"Well, might as well get on with it," she coaxed herself as she slowly sat up in the narrow daybed and swung her feet to the bare floor.

Pulling on a white, seersucker robe, she padded to the bathroom and gingerly tested the faucet. This time it cooperated and ran clear water. She dipped her hands into the cool wetness and splashed her face several times. Drying off with a tattered, but soft towel she felt a bit better, as long as she didn't think.

Brittany knew that sooner or later she was going to have to decide what to do next. But for now she didn't want to think about her next move, her brother or Wolf Light. And she especially didn't want to think about Aren Wulff.

The other thoughts she could put aside with a bit of effort. But no amount of discipline could extinguish the memory of Wulff with his dark head bent over her and his full, sensuous lips descending to meet hers— and the memory of him pulling away.

Young. Vulnerable. Those were the words he had used to describe her.

Was she? Brittany stared at her reflection in the cracked mirror and laid her hairbrush aside.

For years she had thought of herself as a self-assured, mature woman. But the face in the mirror stared back at her with the round, haunted eyes of a lonely child. If she had looked like this last night, no wonder he had pulled away from her.

Oh, God. Why had she done it? Why had she thrown herself into his arms and—

She covered her face with her hands, trying to blot out the shameful memory of how she had kissed him. She had never kissed a man with such total abandon before. And she couldn't understand why she had last night.

Was she really that lonely, that needy? The vision of Wulff's hard, masculine body and handsome face surfaced to offer her solace. Surely any woman would have found it difficult to resist him.

Her reverie was interrupted by a loud knock on the cabin door that made her jump.

Pulling the robe tighter around her, she walked to the door and asked, "Who's there?"

A distinctly male voice replied, "Breakfast."

Brittany opened the door and saw a tall, thin man with a ruddy, freckled complexion and flaming copper hair.

"You're breakfast?" she asked.

He smiled good-naturedly. "I'm Debra's cousin, Bob Wilson. She asked me to bring this to you on my way to work."

He held out a small covered dish to her. "It's something called guava duff. I think it's left over from last night's dinner, but it's good for breakfast, too."

She took the dish, lifted the cover and sniffed the steam that rose from the pastrylike concoction inside.

"Thank you, Bob. You didn't have to do that, but I'm glad you did. It smells great. I think everything you people cook on this island smells great."

Bob leaned his skinny frame against the doorjamb and crossed his arms in front of his chest. "I understand that Aren made you his famous conch chowder last night. Were you able to get it down?"

"Sure. After the first couple of bites my mouth went numb, and the rest was easy. How did you know about that?"

"It's a small island. Everybody knows who had dinner with whom and what they ate." He smiled and added, "Not really, but almost. Jesse told me. He's quite taken with you."

"I'm quite taken with him."

"Wulff or Jesse?"

"Jesse," she answered quickly. Too quickly, she realized when she saw Bob's grin broaden.

"Well, speaking of Wulff, I'd better get going. He sent Jesse down to get me, wants me to work today. Seems he's got something he wants to do. I guess I'll see you later."

"Yes, it was nice meeting you. Thanks for the duff," she called after him as he headed down the beach toward the lighthouse.

Brittany ate her breakfast as quickly as she could, considering that it was very rich and gooey. The flavor was incredible, but she found that she could only eat about half of the pastry.

Then she pulled on a white bikini and a blue terry cloth cover-up.

"Might as well pretend that this is a vacation after all," she murmured to herself as she left the cabin and headed for the beach.

The powder-fine white sand sifted between her toes as she shuffled along the water's edge. Deciding that she didn't have the energy for a swim, she removed her cover-up and spread it on the beach. She sat on it and stared out at the sea for a while.

The waves lapped onto the shore, leaving their white, lacy caps of foam on the sand. The breeze that blew off the waters was much stronger than the previous day's, tossing the fronds of the palm trees that lined the beach behind her. And like the trees she was restless, churning inside with indecision and frustration.

Would Aren really come and try to take her back to Andros this morning? She had been too tired to argue with him when he had said that he would the night before. And he had asked Bob to watch the light for him today because he had something to do.

"Well, let him try," she muttered under her breath. "I'll go back when I get good and ready, and I won't need him to take me when I do."

"What did you say?" asked a small, childish voice behind her.

A black-and-white speckled pup bounded into her lap and began chewing on her fingers with its needle-sharp, puppy teeth.

She turned around to see Jesse in a ragged pair of cut-off jeans, holding a huge kite that was more than twice his size.

"Good morning, Jesse. Good morning, Christopher Columbus," she added, removing her fingers from the puppy's mouth. "What do you have there?"

"This is my pirate kite. It's the best kite in the whole, wide world. See . . ."

The boy stretched the lightweight fabric of the kite on the sand before her and stood, beaming with pride and waiting for her approval.

Brittany didn't disappoint him. "Oh, Jesse, that's a wonderful kite. I've never seen one shaped like a person before. He looks so real."

Jesse pointed out every detail of the pirate's gaudy attire. "He's got a sword and a knife and pistol and a monkey on his shoulder. I like the monkey. I think he's cute, don't you?"

"He's adorable. And I like his red shirt and purple hat, too."

Jesse giggled. "Oh, you're silly. He's not wearing anything except his fur. That's all monkeys wear." He glanced back at the kite. "Oh." He smiled sheepishly. "You mean the pirate."

"Yes, I meant the pirate," she said, tucking her feet beneath her to protect them from the pup's playful but painful nips.

"When you stretch him all out, he's almost as tall as Mr. Wulff."

"Who? The monkey?" she teased.

"No. You *are* silly. I mean the pirate."

"Oh, of course, the pirate. Where did you get such a great kite?"

"Mr. Wulff bought it for me over on Andros when I broke my arm last year. I was climbing a tree." He stopped and reconsidered. "Well, I didn't really break it when I was climbing the tree. I broke it when I fell out of the tree."

"Sounds like you were acting a bit like a monkey yourself."

Jesse laughed. "That's what Mr. Wulff said. I went to see him this morning and boy, was he grumpy. He didn't want to play or nothin'." The child's lower lip protruded in an irresistible pout.

"Sometimes grown-ups have bad days, Jesse," she said gently, stroking the puppy's silky ears as he curled up in her lap for a nap.

"Us kids have bad days, too. But we still like to play."

"Well, that's one of the good things about being a kid. Don't grow up too fast if you can help it."

"Debra says that she's going to tie a brick on my head if I keep growing."

"Good for Debra. How's she feeling this morning?"

"Oh, she's okay. She's kinda grumpy lately, too. I think she's in a hurry for her baby boy to get born, but she's kinda scared, too. I think she's afraid that it's gonna hurt. Is it gonna hurt?"

Brittany looked into the wide, innocent eyes that required complete honesty. "Yes, it'll hurt some. Having a baby is a lot of hard work. But your sister will be fine. As soon as the baby's born, she'll be so happy and relieved that it's over with. Just like when you broke your arm. I'll bet that you cried really hard, huh?"

Jesse nodded vigorously.

"But see, now you're okay. Your arm's all healed and you've got a great kite. Well, Debra will be fine, plus she'll have a beautiful little baby to love and take care of. You're going to have to give her a hand, you know. She'll need all the help she can get."

"I know. Mr. Wulff already told me that, and I'm going to be a really good uncle. I really am."

"I'm sure you will." Brittany recalled the heart-warming scene she had witnessed the evening before from the light keeper's front porch.

She felt an involuntary rush of affection toward this charming, freckle-faced child and the man who cared enough to teach him to read and "throw him overboard." She knew that she would be sorry to see either of them leave her life now that they had entered it.

"Mr. Wulff tells you a lot of good things, doesn't he?" she said.

The boy visibly swelled with pride. "Yeah, he tells me all the important stuff, like how to fly kites and how to wrestle, stuff like that."

"Well, I guess a guy has to learn that stuff sooner or later."

A dark shadow fell across the pirate kite, and a large hand reached out to ruffle Jesse's curls.

"I believe I heard my name mentioned," Wulff said.

Brittany felt her heart lurch at the sound of his deep voice.

She looked up and squinted into the bright light. His massive form was silhouetted against the morning sun, its glittering rays captured in his dark, chestnut waves.

He moved closer to Jesse and dropped to one knee in the sand before the boy. Placing a giant hand on each of the child's shoulders, he looked directly into the wide, amber eyes.

"I'm sorry, Jesse. I shouldn't have yelled at you like that this morning. You didn't do anything wrong. I was in a bad mood, that's all. I guess I must have put my shorts on backward this morning. Do you ever do that?"

Jesse laughed and wrapped his arms around Wulff's neck. "Sure. I put mine on backward a lot, but it don't matter to me, till Granny yells at me."

Wulff grinned and shook him gently. "Your granny just wants you to become a responsible, well-dressed gentleman someday. And gentlemen never ever wear their underwear backward. Isn't that right, Nurse Brittany?"

"No gentleman that I've ever known," she replied solemnly.

Wulff gave her a sideways glance and a smirk that made her giggle.

He turned his attention back to Jesse. "So, old chap, are we okay?"

Jesse reached out and mussed Wulff's hair. In a pretty fair impression of the light keeper's deep voice, he said, "Sure, old chap, just don't let it happen again or we'll make you walk the plank."

Wulff stood and picked the kite up from the sand. "So, you're flying Jolly Roger today."

"Yep, he looked like he was in the mood to fly this morning."

"Well, why don't you take him down the beach a ways there and show us how high he flies."

Jesse looked from Wulff to Brittany. "I know, get lost."

Wulff handed him the kite. "Something like that. You lay low this morning and after we get finished reading this afternoon, we'll arm wrestle. How's that?"

"Oh, good. I'll beat you. I will."

"A puny little bilge rat like you, no way," Wulff called after him as the boy raced down the beach with Jolly Roger trailing behind him.

Wulff sighed, all the levity leaving his face, and dropped down onto the sand beside her. He drew one knee up to his chest and wrapped his arms loosely around it.

He glanced over at Brittany and the sleeping puppy in her lap. "Looks like you're dog-sitting."

"Seems so," she replied tensely.

Why had he come to see her? She was afraid that she knew the answer.

Wulff studied her face carefully. "You don't look so good, kid. What's the matter, didn't you get any sleep at all last night?"

"Not much." She noticed the dark circles under his eyes. The lines seemed deeper across his brow. "You look a bit haggard yourself."

"I spent the night in the lighthouse again."

"There wasn't a storm last night. Was it fog?"

"No, it was a blonde," he replied grudgingly.

"Oh."

"Oh? Is that all you've got to say for yourself? You shouldn't have run off in the dark like that. Him of de hands might have gotten you. If he was lucky," he added, briefly scanning the immediate areas around her bikini.

She reached down and pulled the blue terry cloth around her, moving slowly lest she waken Christopher Columbus, who snored rather loudly, considering his minute size.

"You don't have to get dressed just for me," Wulff said, grinning.

"Yes, I think I do," she replied dryly.

She shivered as his hand glided along her neckline and gently pulled her hair from beneath the robe. Taking longer than necessary, he carefully spread the glittering waves over her shoulders.

"I'm sorry about last night," he murmured. "The fight, that is. I'm not at all sorry about the rest." His eyes lingered on her lips.

"Me, too," she said.

"Do you suppose we could start over?"

"I suppose we could try."

"Good. Hi, I'm Aren Wulff," he said, holding out his hand.

"I'm Brittany Suzanne Davis." She swallowed and added, "Michael's sister."

She put her hand in his and gave him a firm, professional handshake.

"Hey, you took your bandage off," he remarked, turning her hand over and examining her palm.

"I didn't need it anymore. It's doing fine, thanks to some excellent first aid that I received."

He reluctantly released her hand and watched as a pair of gulls circled high above their heads.

"Well, girl," he said, his voice heavy with tension. "Are you all packed up and ready to go?"

"I haven't decided if I'm going or not."

"Haven't decided?" His brows pulled together into an angry scowl. "What the hell does that mean?"

"It seems simple enough to me. I'm not sure that I'm ready to leave yet. That's all."

"Damn it, girl." His heavy brows pulled together over his eyes that flashed with irritation. "I told you that the treasure hunt is off. Why else would you want to stick around this place?"

Her temper flared. "Not that I have to explain my reasons to you," she snapped, "but one of them is Debra. She's going to have her baby any day now, and I told her yesterday that I'd be around if she needs me."

Wulff sighed and lifted his hand to wave absentmindedly to Jesse, who was proudly pointing to his kite as it fluttered and danced on the breeze.

"That's no reason," he argued. "Debra's fine. I'm going to take her over to Andros when she goes into labor, and you don't have to be around for that. I'll take care of it."

Brittany sensed a certain desperate tone in his voice. "What is this?" she asked. "What does it matter to you? I think you're trying to get rid of me."

He shifted uncomfortably and avoided her eyes. "Why would I want to get rid of you?"

"You tell me."

Wulff paused to brush some imaginary grains of sand from his jeans. "Hell, I just think it would be better for you if you left the island right now," he said guardedly. "If you're still serious about this, come back again next summer, and we'll talk about it then."

"Why would anything be different next summer?"

"It just would. Trust me, okay?"

"No, not when you aren't making sense. Besides, this is really important to me, and I want to get it settled."

"What? What's so bloody important to you, girl? What would you do with a fortune if you found one? Buy yourself a mink coat or a string of diamonds? I guarantee you that they wouldn't make you any more beautiful than you already are."

Any other time his compliment would have pleased her. But his scowl told her that flattery was the last thing on his mind. He was very angry with her and she didn't understand why.

"I'm not interested in diamonds or furs," she replied.

"Then why are you doing this?" The desperation had crept back into his voice.

"I'm doing it for Michael."

"Michael? Your brother's dead, sweetheart. How can you do anything for him now?"

She felt the tears spring to her eyes again and blinked them back.

"You don't understand," she said.

His face softened when he saw her unshed tears. "I think you were trying to explain it to me last night and

I cut you off. Please, tell me one more time, and I'll try to understand."

Brittany sighed and dug her bare feet into the white sand. "Do you remember when my mother died? When Michael left his search down here to return to Orlando?"

"Of course I do. Michael and I were close friends back then."

"He came home to take care of me and finish putting me through school."

"I know. You mentioned that last night."

"Well, about a year ago Michael decided to return to the Bahamas and resume his search for our great-grandfather's lost cargo. He wrote and told me that you weren't looking for treasure anymore. He said that you and he had changed, and that the two of you weren't as close as you had been."

A certain sadness flickered across Wulff's face. "That's true. Go on."

"Anyway, he wrote and said that he was having a lot of trouble trying to find it without your help. He had always depended on your knowledge of the island."

Wulff said nothing, but kicked a bit of sand aside with his shoe.

Brittany continued. "And then, I got your telegram, saying that he had drowned in the accident, that he had been drinking and—"

"Drinking?" he interrupted.

"Yes, remember, you said that he was under the influence at the time."

"Oh, yeah." Wulff avoided her eyes. "I'd forgotten that I told you about that. Is that why you don't drink now?"

She waited for the tightness in her chest to go away or at least lighten a bit. "Yes, I can't."

"I understand," he said simply.

They were simple words, but they went straight to her heart. It felt so good to be understood. She placed her hand on the sand between them and he quickly covered it with his own.

There it was again, that overwhelming urge to melt into his arms and absorb his strength. She cursed her weakness and cleared her throat.

"Aren, I haven't thanked you yet for... for making the arrangements to have his body shipped back."

The giant hand tenderly squeezed hers. "That's okay. Michael was my friend. It was the least I could do."

"After the funeral I was so depressed," she said, opening her heart a little more to him. "I felt so bad every time I thought that Michael had never been able to fulfill his dream. He really wanted to find that cargo. It was more than just the monetary value. He felt like it was a part of his past, a part of his father's family that he'd never really known except in the family Bible records. That's when the packet arrived."

Brittany winced at her indiscretion. She hadn't intended to mention that.

"What packet?" he asked fully attentive. She felt the hand that covered hers tense a bit.

"I don't think we'd better talk about that," she said.

"You might as well tell me about it. You don't have much to lose at this point, do you?"

Brittany paused to watch a pair of brown pelicans land clumsily on the swelling tide while she considered his statement. It was true she had little to lose, but Aren Wulff had a great deal at stake. She chose her words carefully. "A couple of months before his death Michael wrote to me and said that he had sent away to a museum in London for some special information from their archives."

"What kind of information?"

"They had a record there of a wrecker's last confession that he gave before they hanged him. He was one of the gang that wrecked my great-grandfather. Michael asked the curator to make copies of the documents and send them to me. He didn't trust your postal service here."

"Wise decision," Wulff replied dryly. "And these records were in the packet that arrived after Michael's death?"

"Yes."

"Well, what did they say?" he prompted.

"They, uh, they said that—"

Wulff's eyes narrowed suspiciously. "Are you getting ready to lie to me again?"

"N-No," she stammered. "I was just thinking. The mooncurser told about wrecking the *Lady Elizabeth*. He said that my great-grandfather Davis made it to shore, he and quite a few of his crew. The wreckers attacked them with clubs and stones, murdered them with their bare hands."

Brittany's voice was thick with emotion. Wulff reached over and rested his hand on her bare knee.

She glanced up at him, startled by the forward gesture at such an inappropriate time. But the look on his face was nothing more than concerned and sympathetic.

"Those were violent times," he said. "Go on."

"After they killed the crew, they pulled the cargo ashore and hid it in one of the caves in Wolf Cove."

"But that's impossible. The light was there by then. My great-grandfather would have seen them hide it. After all, he saw the massacre. In fact, he's the one who turned the bloody buggers over to the authorities."

Brittany glanced down at the sand. "Yes, the record mentioned that, too."

"So, why didn't Captain Wulff see them stash the cargo?"

"How do you know that he didn't?" she asked softly.

"Because Michael and I checked the records over in Nassau years ago. And they said that the cargo was never recovered. Why do you think we spent all that time looking for it when we were young and foolish?"

Brittany sifted a handful of sand through her fingers, letting a few of the sparkling grains fall on the puppy's soft coat.

"Then the stuff is still there in the cove," she whispered.

Wulff sighed and leaned toward her. He put his hand under her chin and lifted her face to his. "Listen to me, girl."

His fingers ran lightly along her trembling jawline. "Are you listening?" he asked. She nodded.

"There are three caves in that cove. Only three. When I was growing up I played by the hour in those caverns. I played pirates in there, I played Tom Sawyer in there, and hell, I even made love for the first time in one of those caves. She was a pretty little blonde who looked a lot like you." He smiled as he watched a blush color her cheeks.

"What I'm trying to tell you is that I'm intimately familiar with those caves. I know every nook and cranny. I found a few things in there over the years, but never anything of real value. If there had been anything, I would have found it.''

"But what about the wrecker's statement? You know, dying man's confession and all of that.''

"I don't know. I can look at it if you want me to. Did you bring the documents with you?''

"Yes," she reluctantly admitted. "But you don't need to do that.''

"I don't mind if it would make you feel better.''

"I would feel better if I could take a look at those caves myself, but I don't suppose you'd do that for me.''

Brittany looked soulfully up into his handsome face, doing what she hoped was a good impression of Christopher Columbus begging. She felt a slight thrill of success when she saw the hard lines in his face melt away.

"If I show you the caves, do you promise to be good and drop this thing once and for all?''

She thought carefully before she answered. "If I can see for myself that what you say is true and that there's no possibility that the cargo could be there, then I promise.''

"And you won't feel too badly about it? Will you know then that you've done everything Michael would have done himself?''

"Yes.''

Wulff stood, took the puppy from her lap and pulled her to her feet. "Then come along, Nurse Brittany. We'll give Jesse his dog and go take a look at the caves. But this is the last time either of us is going to go on a treasure hunt.''

Chapter Five

Stumbling over the jagged cliffs above Wolf Cove, Brittany slipped and struck her knee on a pointed rock.

"Ow," she exclaimed, rubbing the spot. "It's a good thing I changed into jeans before we left."

"Oh, I don't know," Wulff replied. "I kinda liked you the way you were. I don't know when I've seen a bikini filled that nicely."

He offered her his hand as they continued down the rocky slope. "But then, you fill out your jeans rather well, too," he added.

"Just keep your eyes on the trail," she retorted, slipping her hand into his. "That is, if you call this a trail."

"It's a bit rough coming in this way, but it's more scenic, you must admit."

Brittany looked back at the glistening beach they had walked and then ahead at the stony path that led down to the rock-filled inlet. Azure waves crashed onto the rocks, sending a delicate spray of foam into the air. Sea gulls and brown pelicans sunned themselves on the rocks, unimpressed by the turbulence around them.

"Yes, it's beautiful," she admitted. "I'd even say it's worth the climb."

Wulff jumped down a final five-foot drop, reached up and grabbed her around the waist. He slowly lowered her, allowing her body to slide along the length of his before placing her on her feet.

His blue eyes twinkled wickedly beneath their thick, curling lashes. "Yes, I'd definitely say that it's worth the climb."

The desires of the night before flooded over her like liquid fire. Childish vulnerability had nothing to do with it. She longed for the feel of his lips on hers again.

His hands slipped around to her back and pressed her to him. With her breasts crushed against his chest, she could feel the strong, accelerated beat of his heart. And she didn't think it was from the climb.

One of his big hands moved up her back to softly stroke her hair. "Ah, Brittany. Where were you twenty years ago when I needed you?" he murmured.

She looked up at him, grinning impishly. "Kindergarten," she replied.

Wulff sighed and planted a quick, platonic kiss on her forehead. "That's right. I'll try to remember that."

"Don't try too hard," she said smoothly, trailing her fingertips along his rugged jawline.

"You're not making this easy for me." He caught her hand and moved it away from his face.

"I don't want it to be easy. I want it to be hard for you to turn me away."

He pressed a kiss into her palm before dropping her hand. "Well, it's hard. It's very hard."

"Good. Consider that when you're thinking about putting me on a plane to Orlando."

"I have considered it," he said, suddenly looking tired. "I've considered the hell out of it. Come along. The caves are right up here."

They walked along the cove's narrow sandy beach, picking their way among the scattered rocks. Here and there lay weathered pieces of wood and large chunks of iron and other metals rusting in the morning sun.

Ahead, Brittany could see three dark holes in the side of the limestone cliff that surrounded the inlet.

"Are those the caves?" she asked.

"Yep. They're pretty dark inside. Wait here. I'll get some flashlights from the boat house and be right back."

Brittany watched him until he disappeared inside a white building at the mouth of the cove. Then she collapsed onto the warm sand and rubbed the muscles on the back of her neck that were still tight from the stress of the evening before.

Watching the birds that circled above, she wondered if one of them was Harvey. Wulff would probably know, but they all looked alike to her.

A light mist of brine spray settled on her face and in her hair. Licking her lips, she tasted the salty residue and remembered last night's kisses at the top of the light.

The warm memory quickly faded as she surveyed the cove and its jagged rocks . . . the Wolf's teeth. Remembering the records from the museum, she shuddered. This was where it had happened, all those years ago.

Brittany closed her eyes, but her vivid imagination could clearly picture the scene: the blackness of the night, the savage wind, the swollen breakers grinding the ship's hull against the rocks, the horrible sound of wood crushing, splintering on stone.

The men screaming, drowning. And the others fighting their way to shore only to be ruthlessly murdered, their dark blood staining the white sand.

She opened her eyes, but they were flooded with tears. Would there never be an end to her tears? Tears for Michael, and now tears for her ancestor who had died more than a hundred years before. It had been so long ago that it shouldn't matter, but it did.

Strong fingers closed over her shoulder and shook her gently, pulling her back into the present.

Wulff lowered himself onto the sand beside her. His hands moved to cup her face, and he wiped the tears away with his thumbs.

"What is it, Brittany? Why are you crying?"

She looked up into his anxious face and took comfort from his obvious concern. "This...this is the first time I've been in the cove. I've seen it from up there." She gestured toward the lighthouse. "But it's worse, being down here where he died. To actually see the rocks and the waves and to think of him. I just—"

The sob caught in her throat. Instinctively she reached out to Wulff. He pulled her onto his lap as he had done the night before and held her face against his chest.

"I understand, sweetheart," he murmured softly into her hair.

"You do?" she asked, looking up into his eyes. Did he really understand how she, a person with no living family, could grieve for an ancestor that she had never known?

"Of course I do. I know how much you loved Michael."

"Michael?" Startled, she pulled away from his arms. "What do you mean, Michael? I was talking about my great-grandfather Davis."

"Oh, God," Wulff moaned, brushing his hand wearily across his face. "I thought— I'm sorry, honey."

The realization pierced her heart, opening a wound that had barely begun to heal. The cove, those rocks, had devoured her brother as they had killed her great-grandfather.

"No," she cried, pounding her fists against Wulff's broad chest. She didn't even realize that she was hitting him. She was fighting the pain that never ended, that reached out from nowhere to strike her with her guard down.

"Why?" she sobbed. "Why did you lie to me?"

Wulff caught her hands in his and again pulled her into his arms. "I didn't lie to you, Brittany," he said, quietly subduing her. "I told you in the telegram that Michael died at sea. He did."

"But why didn't you tell me that it happened in the cove?"

His hand slid up her throat and he lifted her chin, forcing her to look into his eyes. "Do you feel better now that you know?" he asked softly.

Her lower lip trembled. "No. I feel worse."

"Well, that's why I didn't mention it. I figured that one relative was enough to lose in this cove."

He pulled her head onto his shoulder and began to stroke her hair tenderly.

Brittany wrapped her arms around his waist and laid her cheek against the solid warmth of his chest. She was doing what she had vowed never to do again: cuddling up to him as though he were the father she had never known or the older brother that she had lost.

Was that all he was to her? Was that all she was to him—a lost child?

She closed her eyes and allowed herself the luxury of melting into him, absorbing his strength, his vitality. It didn't matter why she was doing it. Something that felt so right, had to be. Besides, she thought as his fingers laced through her hair and spread it across his chest, he didn't seem to mind too much.

"Wulff?" she whispered.

"Yes, love?"

"Would you hold me for a minute?"

"Ah, girl," he sighed into her hair. "I'd hold you forever if you asked me to."

"See." Wulff shone his flashlight around the jagged stone walls of the cave. "This last one's like the other two, only larger. And it has two rooms."

Brittany followed him as he led her to the back wall of the cavern and through a small round opening that was about two feet across.

The hole was a tight squeeze for Wulff's bulk, but Brittany crawled through easily. She gasped when she saw the size of the inner chamber. It was larger than all of the other caves put together.

The powerful beams from their flashlights illuminated the vast cavern, revealing its walls and ceiling of rocks and hard packed earth.

More stones of all sizes littered the floor, along with bits of rope, pieces of driftwood, some ragged clothing and even a few tin cans.

"Looks like somebody makes themselves at home in here from time to time," she observed, breathing in the dank, musty scent of the chamber.

"Yeah." Wulff kicked an empty soup can aside. "Most of the kids on the island know about this cave. They come in here to play and occasionally to hide out when they're in trouble with their folks."

"And you allow that?"

"Sure. Life's tough for kids. Somebody has to be on their side. Besides, I like children."

"So I noticed." She played her beam along the rocky wall. "I think it's great what you're doing for Jesse."

"Well, hell, somebody's got to do something for him. That no good father of his ran off when he was a little bitty fella. And his mom left him and Debra with that old lady to go get a 'temporary' job on Nassau. That's been three years now, and those kids haven't seen her since. She doesn't even send them any money, and God knows, they're dirt poor."

"Maybe something happened to her." Brittany knelt to examine a stone that caught her eye.

"She's fine. She's working in a posh bar in one of the casinos, making a lot of money. I looked her up last year and gave her a piece of my mind, for all the good it did."

"Well, at least you tried. Wulff, come look at this. What do you think that is?"

He skirted a pile of rags and walked over to stand beside her.

"Well, let's see. Looks a heck of a lot like a rock to me. But then, you never can tell. What do you think?"

"I think you've got a smart mouth. Come on. Look closer. See those scrapes on the side there? They look fresh to me."

Wulff dropped to one knee beside her and closely examined the deep lines in the dirt that was caked onto the side of the stone. Shining his light around the immediate area, he found similar markings on several other rocks.

"Looks like these stones have been moved recently, wouldn't you say?" she asked.

In the dim light she could see the deep furrow of his brow. "Yes, I'd say you're probably right."

"Why do you suppose someone would be moving rocks around in here? Maybe they were hiding something?"

"That's possible," he said a bit gruffly. "Probably the kids messing around, hiding their mom's costume jewelry, or some other great treasure like that. We used to do it all the time."

Brittany couldn't help noticing the tension in his voice and the way he avoided her eyes. He was interested, very interested in the stones, but for some reason he was pretending not to be.

"Come on, Wulff. Look at the size of those rocks. Kids couldn't move them. It must have been an adult."

"So what if it was an adult? What's the big deal?" His tone was defensive and angry.

"I was curious. Aren't you curious why someone would hide something in your cave?"

"Not particularly."

Brittany's eyes searched his and found them cold and guarded. "Now who's lying?" she said.

Wulff stood and walked back toward the small round hole. "Aren't you about ready to leave?" he asked brusquely.

Brittany glanced back at the scraped rocks. "But what about this?"

"What about it? You came in here looking for your great-grandfather's lost cargo. You said yourself that those are fresh markings. They'd have nothing to do with what happened over a hundred years ago, now would they?"

"No, I suppose not," she admitted reluctantly.

"Brittany, you've looked over the caves now. You know that there's nothing here, like I told you." He held out his hand to her and his voice held a pleading note. "Come on, girl, let's go. Please?"

She hesitated for a moment, then rose, walked over to him and took his hand. A hundred questions were on the tip of her tongue, but she swallowed them and allowed him to lead her through the opening and out of the cave.

They stood together on the beach, staring at the waves that crashed on the rocks before them. Although they were joined by clasped hands, a vast desert of silence separated them.

Finally Wulff spoke. "Do you feel like you've done your duty to your brother now?"

"I guess so. I don't know anything else that I can do. I suppose that something could be buried in one of the caves or hidden behind some of those rocks, but I can't very well dig up the floors and burrow into the walls without some more specific information."

"And the record that the museum sent you, it wasn't any more specific than that?"

"No, he said they stashed it in one of the caves. That's all."

Wulff slipped his arm around her shoulders. "I'm sorry, Brittany. I wish I could help you more. But really, you did all you could. Michael would have been satisfied with your effort, I'm sure."

"I don't know, Aren. This meant a lot to Michael, and . . . and I feel as though there's still something left unfinished. That there's more to it."

"Well, I won't argue with you, because I don't know what you're talking about. Did you ever think that your brother would have wanted you to just go on with your own life and lay his memory to rest?"

"No."

"Maybe you should. Why don't you go on back to your cabin, get some rest, lie in the sun and relax for the rest of the day. Tomorrow morning I'll come get you and take you back to Andros. Okay?"

Brittany shrugged his arm off of her shoulders. "Why are you so damned eager to get rid of me?" she demanded.

"I'm . . . I'm not."

"Well, you could have fooled me. Every time I turn around you're trying to take me back to Andros. What are you hiding from me?"

Wulff shuffled the toe of his deck shoe in the white sand.

"And don't lie to me," she said. "I can tell, too, and I don't like it any more than you do."

"All right. I do want you off this island as soon as possible. It's for your own good. I'm sorry, but that's all I can tell you. If you push me any further than that, I'll have to start lying to you. Okay?"

"No, it's not okay." She stared up into his face, which was as hard and fixed as the stone cliff behind him. Clearly no amount of prodding or coaxing would budge him.

"May I ask one question?" she ventured.

"You can ask it. I may not answer it."

"Does this have anything to do with my great-grandfather's lost cargo?"

"Nothing at all," he stated firmly.

"So, it's none of my business, and I just arrived at the wrong time, huh?"

He cleared his throat and ran his fingers through his hair. "Something like that. Would you like me to walk you home?"

"No, I can find my own way. Follow the beach, first cabin on the left. Besides, I have some thinking to do."

Brittany reached out one hand and let it slowly drift down the front of his soft cotton shirt. The warmth of his chest filtered through the thin fabric, causing her to wish that the cloth was gone and her hands were free to wander wherever they wished.

"Answer one more question for me before I go. Is it going to bother you, Aren Wulff, even a little bit, to see me leave tomorrow morning?"

She felt the massive chest beneath her hand heave once, then he clutched her to him.

"Now what the hell do you think?" he asked before his lips took hers.

This time there was no teasing prelude or gentle exploration. His mouth consumed hers with no sign of tenderness, only intense desire.

His left hand supported the back of her head, while his right arm encircled her waist, lifting her, crushing her body against his. Even through their jeans, she could feel the swell of his hard thighs as they pressed against hers.

As his tongue invaded her mouth, drawing soft sighs from her throat, his hand slid from her waist down to cup her hip. Again there was no sense of gentleness, only desire, when his big hand grasped her hip and pulled her pelvis toward his, pressing her to him until his rising need burned against her.

His lips left hers and trailed a path of warm, moist kisses across her cheek to her ear. "So, you think I want to get rid of you, huh?" he whispered gruffly. "Believe me, sweetheart, there's a lot of things I'd love to do to you, and putting you on a plane is not one of them."

Brittany shuddered and ran her fingers through his hair, filling her hands with the thick, soft curls.

"Then don't, Aren. Don't send me away," she pleaded.

Wulff released his hold on her and stepped back, surveying what he had relinquished. Gradually he regained his breath and his composure. "Did you get sand in your sneakers?" he asked.

"Did I what?"

"Did you get sand in your shoes?"

"Well, of course I got sand in my shoes. I was walking on the beach."

"Then you'll come back to me someday, Nurse Brittany. We have a saying in the Bahamas that if you get sand in your shoes, you have to return to the islands. Now run along. Get out of here while I still have the strength to do the right thing and let you go."

* * *

"Debra, are you here?" Brittany quickly scanned the small store. There was no sign of the expectant red-head.

"Yes, I'm over here," came a weak voice from somewhere in the corner.

Brittany peeked around the end of the counter and saw the girl seated on a rough-hewn crate with her arms wrapped around her abdomen.

"What are you doing there, honey? Are you all right?"

"I guess so," Debra replied. "I'm having these cramps again."

"What kind of cramps?"

"Oh, my belly sort of bunches up and squeezes."

Brittany walked around the counter and knelt beside her. "Does it hurt?" she asked.

"Not really, it just feels kinda funny."

Debra winced and again clutched her stomach.

"Are you having one right now?"

"Yeah, it just started."

She placed her hand on the girl's abdomen and looked at the second hand on her watch.

"It's gone now, isn't it?" she said.

"Yeah. It comes and goes like that."

Brittany consulted her watch again. "It only lasted ten seconds. Is that about how long they've been?"

"Yeah, they don't last very long. Sometimes I have a bunch in a row, then I don't have any for the rest of the day."

"How long have you been having them?"

The girl smoothed the wrinkles in the front of her denim smock with a freckled hand. "Oh, off and on for the last couple of weeks."

"Well, I don't think they're real labor pains, yet. They're what you call Braxton-Hicks contractions."

Debra's brown eyes widened in alarm. "Those sound awful. Are they?"

Brittany laughed and patted the girl's shoulder soothingly. "No, not at all. Your muscles are just practicing for the big event. It's perfectly normal." She moved her hand to the swollen belly. "May I?" she asked.

"Sure, go ahead."

Gently examining the girl's drum-tight abdomen, she said, "You don't have a lot of room left in there, do you?"

"Not even enough to eat a full meal anymore."

"Or even breathe?"

Debra laughed. "Yeah, or even breathe. I'll sure be glad when this is over."

"Well, it feels like the baby's head is right down there ready to go. Sounds like mommy's ready, too."

The redhead smiled a warm, toothsome grin and nodded. "I've had my suitcase packed for months. And a friend of my grandma's gave me a white bassinet for the baby to sleep in. And I've got some little clothes for him."

Brittany lowered herself onto another crate beside Debra and rested her chin in her hands. "So, do you think it's going to be a boy, too?"

"It has to be, or Jesse's going to be really disappointed."

"Are you looking forward to the baby as much as Jesse is?"

Debra's grin broadened and her eyes sparkled with anticipation. "Oh, yes, I love babies. I took care of Jesse for my mom when he was born. I know about diapers and bottles and all that stuff. But I'd like to nurse my baby, if I can. Have you ever had a baby?" the girl asked timidly.

"No, but I worked in maternity for two years, and I helped a lot of other women have theirs."

"I bet they weren't as young as me."

"Yes, Debra, some of them were, and they did fine." Brittany patted the work roughened, speckled hand. "You'll be all right, I promise."

The girl looked away, as though unaccustomed to tenderness. "I was going to ask you something, but I don't know if I should or not."

"What were you going to ask?"

"I was wondering if...if you would go with me over to Andros when Mr. Wulff takes me there. I know it's a lot to ask, but—"

Brittany was touched by the girl's trust and humility. "Not at all. I'd be delighted to go with you. I was thinking about leaving the island tomorrow morning, but I'll stay until your baby's born. I didn't really want to leave yet anyway. I don't feel like I've finished what I came here for."

Debra winced again and patted her belly. "He's wiggling all around in there. I guess he doesn't like getting squeezed like that. I forgot to ask you—why have you come to Wolf Island?"

"I have some business to take care of." She hesitated, deciding whether or not to confide in the girl. "Did you know Michael Davis?"

"Sure, I knew Mike. Hey, your name is Davis. He wasn't related to you, was he?"

"Yes, he was my brother?"

Debra's amber eyes widened with surprise, even a bit of shock. "Really? You're kidding!" Then she glanced away uncomfortably. "Oh, I'm sorry. It must have been awful for you, Mike getting killed like that. Bob felt really bad that he couldn't rescue him."

"Bob? Where was Aren?"

"Mr. Wulff had gone to Nassau that night. He'd left Bob in charge of the lighthouse. Bob saw Michael wreck there on the rocks, but he wasn't able to pull him out of the water in time. The waves threw him into the rocks and smashed his..."

The girl hesitated, embarrassed by her indiscretion and the look of pain on Brittany's face. "But you already knew that."

Brittany felt as though an icy hand was gripping her heart, squeezing it to see if there were any more tears left.

No, she hadn't known that. When Michael's remains had arrived in Orlando, she had refused to view the body. Wulff had already made the positive identification with the Bahamian coroner.

She hadn't asked the exact cause of death; she didn't want to know. Her eyes had caught the words "massive brain contusion" on the death certificate, and that was as much information as she had dared subject herself to at the time.

Brittany had known all too well the delicacy of her own mental state and had carefully shielded herself from anything that would cause her pain to be any more acute.

But here on Wolf Island the facts were everywhere, suddenly appearing without warning, catching her with her defenses down. She wasn't sure that she could bear the realities of her brother's death.

Brittany gulped and swallowed the lump in her throat. Yes, she decided, she could face it now. Time had passed and she was stronger. Now was the time to conquer her grief, once and for all.

A delicate brass bell jingled as someone walked in the door.

"Hello, anybody here?" inquired a cheerful, male voice.

"Over here," Debra announced.

Bob leaned his long, skinny frame over the countertop and said, "So, sittin' down on the job again, huh, Deb."

He glanced at Brittany. "You're supposed to be waiting on the customers, cousin, not visiting with them."

"Oh, shut up, Red. Who asked ya?" Debra said, shuffling her feet.

Bob turned to Brittany. "She's sure been cranky lately. I'll be glad when she has that baby. Maybe then we can get some service around here."

"I'm not going to wait on you," Debra snapped. "You can find what you need, and you know where I keep the cash box. Wait on your own self."

Bob shook his head and clicked his tongue. "Cranky I tell you, cr-an-ky."

"Don't give me a hard time. Miss Davis says that I'm going to be a mommy any day now and she should know, she's a nurse."

"Did you say Davis?" Bob asked, his smile disappearing.

"Yes, I'm Michael's sister."

The young man hung his head and shoved his hands deep into the pockets of his khakis. "I'm ... I'm really sorry about your brother," he stammered.

"Thank you. Debra was telling me that you tried to rescue him. I want you to know that I really appreciate your effort."

"That's nice of you to say, but obviously it wasn't enough. I wish that Wulff had been there instead of me that night. He probably could have saved him."

"Don't say that. I'm sure you did exactly what he or anyone else would have done."

"Yes, well, I guess we'll never know for sure. I think it'll haunt me till the day I die."

He folded his long, thin arms across his chest. "I've got to go. I just came by to see if you have any fresh milk."

"You know where it is," Debra said. "Help yourself."

Brittany rose and started toward the door. "I'm going to go, too. I want to lie in the sun a little more and maybe take a nap. Then this evening I'll ride up to the light and tell Aren that I'm not leaving, so that he won't make an unnecessary trip down here in the morning." She stopped and turned. "On second thought, Debra, maybe I should stick around in case you need me."

Bob tossed a couple of coins into the metal cash box. "That's okay. I live right next door to her. If she starts getting frisky, I'll run up and get you."

"Is that all right?" she asked the girl.

"Sure, that's fine. Tell Mr. Wulff 'hi' for me and tell him to get his boat ready to go."

Chapter Six

Brittany climbed the last few steps of the spiraling staircase, entered the lantern chamber of the lighthouse and looked around. She seemed to be having trouble finding people today.

Wulff hadn't answered the door when she had rung the brass bell on the porch, so she decided to look for him in the light tower. But he wasn't there either, she discovered when she found the top of the light empty except for the glistening Fresnel lens.

Brittany opened the door and walked out onto the narrow, iron balcony. Once again, she inhaled the pungent aroma of the sea.

Yesterday's gentle breeze had become an insistent wind that whipped her hair around her shoulders and across her face. On the distant horizon a bank of dark clouds gathered ranks.

Slowly circling the tower, she began to notice something unique about the shape of Wolf Island. Before, she had been so occupied with Aren and the individual sights and sounds of the island that she had failed to view it as a whole. From where she stood, she could clearly see that, like Aren's tattoo and the sign, the island was shaped like the profile of a wolf.

Thrilled with her discovery, Brittany studied the outline of the island's shores and saw that the village covered the back of the wolf's head. His ears formed another cove, much the same shape and size as Wolf Cove.

Appropriately, the lighthouse was the eye and directly below her lay the gaping mouth filled with its razor sharp teeth.

As she looked down, a movement caught her attention. Someone was coming out of one of the caves. She moved along the rail until she could get a better look. It was Wulff and a short, heavyset, bald man whom she hadn't seen before.

They were deeply engrossed in conversation, and although she couldn't be sure from such a distance, they seemed to be arguing. Wulff shook his head vigorously several times, and the stocky fellow made several violent gestures toward the cove.

Even though she couldn't hear a word they were saying, Brittany instinctively didn't like Wulff's paunchy companion. She reminded herself that it was ridiculous to make a judgment about his character on appearances alone.

But there was something aggressive and hostile about the man's body stance and motions that made her suspicious of him. What she could see of his face looked hard, almost sinister to her.

Why would Aren be talking to someone like that? she wondered. He certainly didn't appear to be enjoying himself.

At one point Wulff shook his head, shrugged and walked away. The bald man followed him up the trail and grabbed the light keeper's brawny forearm.

Brittany watched as Wulff grasped the man's wrist and peeled it away from his arm. She saw the fellow rub his hand after Aren released it and she smiled, remembering the pain from that grip. Served him right.

The two men talked for another minute or two before the man left Wulff and strode toward the boat house and a heavy, clumsy looking motorboat that was tied there.

Wulff watched the man until he had left the cove. Then he started slowly up the path toward the lighthouse, his head down, his hands thrust deeply into his pockets.

Brittany heard him open the steel door at the base of the tower and waited anxiously for him to reach the top of the stairs.

She watched through the glass as he entered the lantern chamber. His handsome features were drawn into a grim expression of anger and worry. He looked like a man who had fought an important battle. And lost.

But the second his eyes caught hers, they lit with delight at seeing her. She waved and, to her own amazement, blew him a kiss through the window.

In a moment he was on the balcony beside her, his hands encircling her waist.

A rush of adrenaline flooded through her as his hands tightened around her possessively.

"Hot damn!" he exclaimed. "I didn't think I'd get to see you again until tomorrow morning."

"I thought you might want some company this evening," she said. Her hands succumbed to temptation and trailed up his arms to his shoulders.

He wore a close-fitting, black tank top, cut deeply at the neck and around the arms, leaving his shoulders and a large part of his chest bare. Her fingers glided over his smooth, warm skin, savoring the hardness of the muscles that lay below the surface.

Wulff felt his insides quiver as her soft fingers wound themselves in the hair at the back of his neck.

The effect that this girl had on him was devastating. She could do more to arouse him with a single touch than most women did with . . . much more.

There was such a delicate air of fragility about her, a certain innocence. But gazing into her golden eyes, he saw a look that was anything but innocent.

She wanted him as much as he wanted her. And God, how he wanted her.

Every time he saw her, every time he touched her, it became more difficult to remember that she was only a girl, Michael's little sister, Susie.

Her fingertips lightly brushed his lower lip, and he felt a muscle spasm deep in his loins. Yes, it was getting very hard to remember why he shouldn't touch her.

His hand slid beneath the soft fabric of her blouse and waited, giving her time to object. Instead, she stepped closer to him, her eyes warm and inviting.

Wulff moved his hand slowly along her midriff, delighting in the exquisite velvet of her skin. He felt her tremble as he tenderly cupped the lace-covered underside of her breast, allowing it to lie in his hand, warm and heavy in its fullness.

He longed to reach inside the lace and explore the delicate skin that he somehow knew would be the softest he had ever touched.

But Wulff knew that if he continued to indulge himself, he would take her, right there on the balcony. And that wasn't what he wanted.

What the hell did he want from her? The question churned through his already agitated insides, causing him to withdraw his hand and step away from her.

He wanted to make love to her more than he had ever wanted anything before. Since they had first kissed he had thought of little else than how it would feel to have her soft hands caress and stroke his body.

It was a fantasy that had consumed his every waking moment and had even invaded his sleep, sending him to the top of the tower in the middle of the night, rather than lie in bed alone without her.

He looked down at her, standing there with her heart in her eyes, and wondered why he didn't just go ahead and take what she was offering. She was so damned beautiful. No, Nurse Brittany was much more than that. She was intelligent, funny, sensitive and caring. And those were his favorite qualities in a person . . . in a woman . . . more specifically, in a wife.

Grudgingly, Wulff faced the thought that had been nagging at him: the dream of finding a wife. Years ago he had decided that he was too picky when it came to choosing someone to share his life with. Even if he had found a woman that he wanted, he would have been reluctant to ask her to marry him.

Being a lighthouse keeper's wife was more than a relationship; it was a job, a job that required strength, courage and, occasionally, great sacrifice. Wulff had never forgotten the price that his mother had paid, and he wasn't sure he could ask that of a woman he loved.

A woman he loved? Did he love her? He looked down at her shining hair and her soft smile. He remembered her gentle way with Jesse when he had watched them together on the beach that morning and the fire in her kisses the night before.

Yes, he was pretty sure he did love her.

But was Nurse Brittany Davis the kind of woman who could be a lighthouse keeper's wife? He glanced over her slight form and searched her big, golden eyes. No, of course not. After all, she was only a girl.

"Hey. Hey, you."

Her voice invaded his thoughts and brought him back to reality.

"What?"

She laughed and slipped her hand into his. "You were way out in left field. What were you thinking about?"

Wulff twisted one of her curls around his finger. "I was thinking that I like long hair."

She looked at him doubtfully. "What else?"

"That I like long, blond hair."

"Come on, Wulff."

He sighed and gathered a handful of the golden silk. "All right, I was thinking that I like *your* long, blond hair. Satisfied?"

"No, but it's all right. If you don't want to tell me, say so."

He chuckled and pulled a strand of her hair across her upper lip, giving her a mustache. "Okay, I don't want to tell you."

Exasperated, she pushed his hand away and leaned forward, placing both elbows on the railing. "You're a complicated man, Aren Wulff."

He leaned his back against the banister and crossed his arms. "Not really. I have the same basic needs that any other man has."

Brittany hung her head, her hair falling around her face. "Then why did you stop?" she asked quietly.

"What?"

"A moment ago, when we were—"

"I stopped then because I knew that if I went any further I wouldn't be able to stop. I care for you, Brittany. And I don't want our first time to be out here on the balcony. Maybe our fifth . . . or sixth . . . or . . ."

She looked up and saw him smiling at her, his eyes crinkling into tiny lines at the corners.

"And what makes you so sure that we're going to have a first time . . . or a sixth?"

"I can tell you right now, if you keep touching me and looking at me like you've been doing, we're going to be having that first time pretty soon. You're playing havoc with my physical constitution."

Brittany grinned playfully, then glanced away, her face turning a delicate pink.

"Well," he said, "aren't you going to tell me what thought produced that lovely blush?"

"An unladylike thought, to be sure," she admitted. "Something about playing with your physical constitution."

"Oh, Lord," he moaned, running his fingers through his hair. "I can't take much more of this. Come on."

He took her arm and led her toward the door. "Let's see if we can find something in the kitchen for dinner.

It'll be dark in a little while and the wind's picking up.
I have a feeling that I'm going to be on watch at least
part of the night.''

She brushed against him as she passed through the
door, setting off tremors throughout his body that
eventually settled in his groin.

"Not that I could have gotten any sleep anyway," he
added with a sigh.

"Even your leftovers are great," Brittany said as she
sank deep into the cushions of the sofa.

Wulff stood, looking out the window at the palms
that whipped about in the face of the wind. "I'm glad
you enjoyed them," he replied absentmindedly. "You
know, it's blowing up a pretty good one out there."

"Do you think it'll rain?"

"Not necessarily. We might just have heavy winds
and high tides. Either way, I think you'd better consider staying the night. It would be a bit rough getting
down the hill unless you absolutely had to. I have a
guest room," he added.

"But what if Debra needs us?"

He left the window and walked over to sit beside her
on the sofa. "Didn't you say that Bob will come get us
if she does?"

"Yes, but—"

He laid one finger across her lips. "Stop worrying,
Nurse Brittany. She probably won't go into labor this
evening. At least, we'd better hope she doesn't. With
the sea as choppy as it is, I wouldn't risk taking her to
Andros anyway." His finger hooked beneath her chin
and lifted her face to his. "Could you deliver the baby
if you had to?"

"Sure, if I had to. But I'd rather have her in a clinic in case of complications."

"Well, we won't worry about it now. Like Jesse's granny says, 'Don't trouble trouble till trouble troubles you.'"

"Huh?"

"Never mind."

"Do you need to go up into the light yet?" she asked, propping her feet beside his on the old chest.

"Not for a little while. We can sit here and digest for a few more minutes until it's dark. So, kid," he said nudging her foot with his, "are you ready to go tomorrow morning if this storm has cleared?"

"Actually, that's what I came up here to tell you. I promised Debra this afternoon that I'd stay until her baby's born. She wants me to go with her over to Andros." Brittany paused to take a breath and wait for his angry response.

Instead he seemed relieved, maybe even a bit pleased. "Whatever you say. You're the nurse."

"Aren't you even going to give me your usual, vague argument about getting on with my life?"

"No," he replied. "If I were a better man, I would. But you've worn down all of my honorable intentions."

"All?" she asked mischievously.

"Nearly all," he qualified.

"Would that fellow that you were talking to down in the cove today have anything to do with you wanting me to leave the island?"

Wulff looked stunned. "Why the hell would you ask something like that?"

"Because I had an uneasy feeling about him. And judging from the look on your face, I'd say that I was right."

"You and your blasted feelings," he growled. "You're too smart for your own good, girl."

"So, what does that guy have to do with me?"

"Nothing. Not a bloody thing. He's not someone that you have to concern yourself with. I've got him under control."

"From where I stood, it looked like he was controlling you, or at least trying to."

"You ask too damn many questions," he said, moving closer to her. "And there's only one way I know to shut you up."

His right arm, which had been resting on the back of the sofa, wrapped around her shoulders and pulled her against him. His left hand found the curve of her waist and rested there before inching its way up her midriff. Her breasts ached for his touch. She felt her nipples harden with anticipation the way they had earlier on the balcony.

"Now who's starting something?" she whispered as she lifted her lips to his.

"It's okay. I have to go up in the light in a few minutes, so I won't have time to finish it."

His mouth descended on hers, stealing her breath away with its gentle, but firm demands. Obediently her lips parted, allowing him inside, where her tongue met his in an exchange of tender intimacies.

For what seemed like an eternity his mouth took hers, drawing what he needed from her. She drank in his passion and then returned it to him, magnified by her own needs and desires.

Her hands sought the dark, curling hair on his chest and found it as soft and lush as she had hoped. When she touched him every discovery was as satisfying and fulfilling as her fantasies, or even more.

Meanwhile, Wulff was making sweet discoveries of his own. His hand left her ribs and again cupped the underside of her breast, lifting it until its top swelled into the neckline of her shirt.

He groaned at the sight of the rounded, creamy globe that lured him to lower his head and taste its softness.

His tongue traced hot, silken swirls that dipped lower and lower into her cleavage until it reached the edge of her bra.

He hesitated, wanting to strip away the lacy barrier and grant his tongue and lips the feast they craved. But Wulff knew that if he crossed that line, there would be no turning back.

Brittany waited, sensing his turmoil, drowning in her own. She, too, wanted to pull away the offending fabric and press his head to her breast, holding him there until she had had enough. But she knew that it wouldn't be enough.

With a shuddering sigh he lifted his face from her chest and buried it in her hair. "God help me, Brittany," he murmured. "I'm afraid that I'm in love with you."

She laid her head on his shoulder. "Well, if love is something to be afraid of, we're both in deep trouble," she said.

"Really?" He lifted his face from her hair and searched her eyes.

"Of course. Surely you knew—"

He watched her finger trace the outline of the wolf's head on his arm. "I suspected."

"So, what do you intend to do about it?"

He bent down and lingeringly kissed her cheek and forehead. "Well, for right now I'm going to go fight my way through the wind up to the light. Then I'm going to keep watch until it lets up a bit." His eyes scanned her lips and her breasts, which were still rosy from the abrasion of his beard. "And I'm going to eat my heart out. Do you want me to show you to your room now, or would you like to come along?"

"May I?"

"If you promise to be good."

"Good? I'd be very good if you'd let me," she purred.

"Yes, I'll bet you would. Maybe I'd better rephrase that. You have to promise to—"

A loud, insistent pounding on the door startled them both.

"Bloody hell. Who'd be out on a night like this?" Wulff exclaimed, rushing to the door.

"Oh, no, I hope it's not...Bob," Brittany exclaimed as the skinny redhead nearly fell headlong through the open doorway.

Wulff had to press his shoulder to the door to close it against the wind.

"Don't tell me, the girl's in labor?" he asked his assistant, whose flaming red hair stood on end and whose clothes hung haphazardly on his scrawny frame.

"Well, I didn't come up here in this storm to wish you a good evening." He bent over and gasped for breath, his face a mottled red from exertion.

"She's been having those pains for a couple of hours, but she wouldn't let me come up here to get you until she was sure it was the real thing. She's sure now. She's yelling and everything. What are we going to do?''

Wulff turned to Brittany. ''We can't take her to Andros, that's for sure. I can get you down the hill if you can deliver the baby.''

Brittany jumped to her feet, her heart in her throat. ''Let's go. I'm ready when you are.''

''I'll stay here and watch the light,'' Bob volunteered.

''Good. Do we need to take anything with us?'' Wulff asked.

''Let me see that wonderful first-aid kit of yours. There might be something in there I can use.''

Quickly Wulff hauled the case out of the mahogany cupboard and laid it open on the table for her inspection.

She chose cotton balls, a roll of gauze, scissors, alcohol and antiseptic soap.

''No surgical gloves, huh?'' she asked, searching through the case.

''Sorry, but I don't have much need for them. Here's a bag for that stuff and a sweater for you.''

She quickly donned the huge sweater that he proffered, and stuffed the paper bag of supplies into one of its deep pockets.

''Let's get going,'' she said. ''Debra probably won't deliver for hours, but we still need to get there as quickly as we can.''

When they opened the door the wind nearly knocked Brittany to her knees.

''Good heavens,'' she cried as Wulff grabbed her around the waist. ''Are we going to make it down there in this?''

He leaned over and shouted in her ear, "We'll make it. Come on, this way."

With their heads bent into the wind, he led her around the house to a small shed. They rushed inside, grateful for the moment's respite from the gusts that stole their breath away and brought stinging tears to their eyes.

In the darkness of the shed Brittany could see the outline of a large object covered with a white cloth. Wulff ripped the covering away and revealed a huge, gleaming, black motorcycle.

"A Harley?" she asked incredulously. "You've got a Harley-Davidson on this island?"

"Comes in handy from time to time. Like now."

He threw one leg over the motorcycle, and after several kick starts, the engine roared to life. He patted the seat behind him. "Come along, Nurse Brittany," he shouted. "Your ambulance awaits."

She climbed on behind him and wrapped her arms around his waist.

"Hang on," he yelled in her ear. "I don't want to lose you."

Brittany plastered herself against his back and gripped him even tighter. "You won't. Let's go."

The bike leaped beneath them, and they hurtled down the dark, bumpy road toward the village.

Chapter Seven

A faint yellow light glowed from the window of the limestone cottage as Wulff maneuvered the Harley near the door and killed the engine. When they climbed off the motorcycle and hurried toward the cabin, Brittany noticed that either the wind had died down a bit since they had left Wolf Rock or it wasn't blowing so hard in the village.

But even here the roar of the surf and the whistle of the wind as it rounded the corner of the house made communication difficult.

"We made it," she shouted into Wulff's ear as he bent his head down to hers and wrapped his arm around her shoulders.

"I told you I'd get you here," he said, giving her a squeeze. "Did you doubt me?"

"Not really."

"So, now that you're here, can you handle this situation?" he asked, pounding his fist on the door.

"Sure. Do you doubt me?"

In the dim light he searched her upturned face for signs of insecurity or inadequacy and found only a quiet sense of self-confidence.

"No. I don't doubt you, Nurse Brittany. It's just that I really care about Debra and Jesse. They're like my own kids, you know."

Brittany smiled. "Yes, I know. Don't worry, Uncle Aren, it'll be all right."

The door opened and Jesse stood there, gazing up at them with a woeful look on his freckled face, his bottom lip trembling.

"Oh, Mr. Wulff, Miss Davis, I'm glad you're here. Deb's feeling awful bad. I think she's gonna die."

Wulff lifted the boy into his arms and said, "Hey, mate. Don't talk like that. You know we're not going to let your sister die. Come on, let's see her."

Brittany followed them into the cottage, where the first thing she saw was their grandmother, sitting in a rattan rocking chair in the corner. A pink robe of tattered chenille was wrapped about her and her gnarled, arthritic hands were folded in her lap.

A kerosene lamp glowed atop a citrus crate in the corner behind the old lady. Its feeble light did little to dispel the gloom of the bare, cheerless room. The only other pieces of furniture were the borrowed bassinet in the corner and a threadbare, tweed sofa.

Debra lay on the couch, her face white with pain and fear, her breathing rapid and shallow.

Brittany rushed to her side, knelt on the worn, gray linoleum and wiped the sweat away from the girl's forehead. "How are you doing, sweetheart?" she asked.

Debra burst into tears and covered her face with her hands. Brittany turned to the grandmother who calmly rocked back and forth in her chair.

"How far apart are her contractions?" she asked the old woman.

"Eh?" She cupped her hand to her ear.

"How far apart are the pains?" Brittany shouted.

"Yeah, she's pretty bad off...the wages of sin," she mumbled and nodded her head knowingly. "The wages of sin is death."

The old woman resumed her rocking, her eyes and attention fixed upon an insect that was slowly crawling up the wall.

"Yes, well." Brittany sighed. Grandma was going to be loads of help.

"Debra, look at me." She pulled the girl's hands away from her face. "Listen to me, okay?"

The little redhead stopped crying and looked up at the woman who held her hands. "Yes," she gasped between hiccuping sobs.

"You and your baby are going to be fine. Mr. Wulff and I are going to take care of you. Do you understand?"

"Yes, but...Bob said that we can't go to Andros, 'cause the wind's too bad," she wailed.

"That's true. But we don't have to go to Andros. You can have your baby right here at home. I'll deliver it and Mr. Wulff can help. Is that okay?"

Debra glanced doubtfully from Brittany to Wulff, who stood behind her, still holding Jesse in his arms.

"Nurse Brittany is a damn good nurse, Deb," Wulff said solemnly. "I hear she's the best in the hospital where she works. I wouldn't worry a bit if she was taking care of me."

"Okay. It's okay then. Thank you," the girl said, looking up at him, with youthful trust shining in her eyes. "Oh! Oh no, here it comes again."

Her brown eyes grew wide with fear as the contraction began. Brittany placed her hands on the girl's abdomen and looked at her watch.

"Just relax, Debra, relax and let it go. It's all right."

With gentle, soothing words she talked the girl through the contraction. When it was over she looked at her watch. Sixty-two seconds.

"Well, I think we've got a ways to go yet, Debra," she said. "Why don't we make you as comfortable as possible. Aren, would you help me get her into the bedroom?"

Wulff stood Jesse on his feet and moved over to the sofa. "Oh, I don't know," he said, smiling down at Debra. "I used to carry you around on my shoulders all the time, but you've put on a bit of weight in the past twelve years."

He lightly scooped her into his arms and turned to Brittany. "Well, where do you want me to dump her?"

"You didn't have to pick her up. She can still walk at this point."

Wulff groaned with exaggerated effort. "Now you tell me."

Debra smiled weakly and wrapped her arms around his neck as he carried her into the bedroom and gently laid her on the bed.

Brittany followed them and quickly checked out the cramped room. The rough, plastered walls were whitewashed, their only decoration being a couple of faded religious pictures and mementoes. Jesse's pirate kite, propped in the corner, was the only bright spot in the dismal surroundings.

Debra lay on a double bed that was shoved against the wall. Beside the bed was a small round table with the ever-present kerosene lamp.

Brittany lit the lamp and instantly disapproved of its faint light and strong kerosene smell.

"Do you suppose we can have some more light in here?" she asked Wulff.

He hesitated. "I could bring the lamp out of the living room, but that would leave Grandma and Jesse in the dark."

"They don't have any extras?" she asked.

He glanced over at Debra and lowered his voice. "I doubt it. Lamps are expensive to light and Grandma is, uh, frugal."

"Well, now's no time for frugality. There's one in my cabin, if you would get it. And I'll need all the clean towels and sheets you can find, some boiling water for sterilizing, a large bowl with fresh water in it and some washcloths. Got that?"

He counted the items off on his fingers. "Got it," he said and disappeared from the room.

Brittany pulled the small table to the foot of the bed and carefully laid out the items that she had brought with her from Wulff's case.

A groan came from the bed and she turned to see Debra clutch her stomach, her face contorting with pain. Brittany left the table and sat beside the girl on the bed. Taking Debra's hands in hers, she said, "Honey, breathe like this. Come on, do it. I promise it'll help."

As the contraction gathered strength the girl clung to her hands and imitated the breathing pattern.

"That's it—in your nose and out your mouth. There you go. Keep it going."

She looked at the second hand on her watch. "You're doing great. It's almost over now. There. That wasn't so bad, was it?" She wiped the amber curls away from the sweaty brow.

"No," the girl gasped, rolling her head back on the pillow. "That was better."

"Good. That's what we're going to do every time. We're going to breathe like that, and you're going to be able to stay on top of those contractions instead of them getting on top of you. Okay?"

The girl nodded, gradually releasing her tight grip on Brittany's hand.

"All right. You rest now until the next one."

Brittany looked up to see Wulff standing in the doorway, his arms full of towels, sheets and the hurricane lamp from her cabin. He was smiling at her, a soft, affectionate smile that was tinged with something like admiration.

"I see you got my stuff. Thanks." She took the towels and sheets from him.

"I see you've got things under control," he said, nodding toward Debra. "Thanks, Nurse Brittany."

"You're welcome, but we're not exactly home free. It's going to be a long night, and I'm afraid we're not going to be getting much help from Grandma."

"I could have told you that," he said, shaking his head.

"Have you ever helped with a delivery before?"

"No, I'm afraid not."

"Ever seen a birth?"

"Do kittens and puppies count?"

"Not really."

◆§ IT'S A §◆

SILHOUETTE HONEYMOON

A SWEETHEART

OF A FREE OFFER!

FOUR NEW SILHOUETTE SPECIAL EDITION NOVELS—FREE!

Take a "Silhouette Honeymoon" with four exciting romances—yours FREE from Silhouette Special Edition. Each of these hot-off-the-press novels brings you all the passion and tenderness of today's greatest love stories…your free passport to a bright new world of love and adventure! But wait…there's <u>even more</u> to this great offer!

SPECIAL EXTRAS—FREE!

You'll get your free quarterly newsletter, packed with news on your favorite writers, upcoming books, even recipes from your favorite authors.

MONEY-SAVING HOME DELIVERY!

Send for your Silhouette Special Edition novels and enjoy the <u>convenience</u> of previewing six new books every month, delivered right to your home. If you decide to keep them, pay just $2.50 per book— with no additional charges for home delivery. Great savings plus total convenience add up to a sweetheart of a deal for y<u>ou</u>!

START YOUR SILHOUETTE HONEYMOON TODAY— JUST COMPLETE, DETACH & MAIL YOUR FREE OFFER CARD!

FILL OUT THIS POSTPAID CARD AND MAIL TODAY!

SILHOUETTE

SPECIAL EDITION®

FREE OFFER CARD

FREE!

FREE HOME DELIVERY!

4 FREE BOOKS

PLUS AN EXTRA BONUS MYSTERY GIFT!

☐ **YES!** Please send me my four SILHOUETTE SPECIAL EDITION novels, _free_, along with my free Mystery Gift! Then send me six new SILHOUETTE SPECIAL EDITION novels every month, as they come off the presses, and bill me just $2.50 per book with no extra charges for shipping and handling. If I am not completely satisfied, I may return a shipment and cancel at any time. The free books, and Mystery Gift remain mine to keep!   54CI1186

NAME _____
(please print)

ADDRESS _____ APT. _____

CITY _____

PROV./STATE _____ POSTAL CODE/ZIP _____

Terms and prices subject to change. Your enrollment is subject to acceptance by Silhouette Books.
SILHOUETTE SPECIAL EDITION is a registered trademark.

PRINTED IN U.S.A.

**Business
Reply Mail**

No Postage Stamp
Necessary if Mailed
in Canada

Postage will be paid by

**SILHOUETTE BOOK CLUB
OF CANADA**
320 STEELCASE RD. E.
MARKHAM, ONTARIO
L3R 9Z9

Canada Post Postes Canada

374

"Then no."

"You aren't going to throw up or faint on me, are you?"

He grinned mischievously. "No, Nurse Brittany. I've never thrown up on a lady yet."

"You know what I mean."

"Yes, I know what you mean." He lit the other lamp and replaced the glass chimney. "I'll do whatever you tell me to do, when you tell me to do it. Then, when it's all over, I'll go outside and quietly pass out."

"What more could I ask? Oh, here we go again."

For the next two hours Brittany sat beside her patient, holding her hand, rubbing her back, bathing her forehead with a damp washcloth and breathing with her through the pains that grew progressively longer and more intense.

Wulff stood quietly in the corner, watching, saying nothing. He listened as the woman's calm, gentle voice soothed the girl and gave her the courage to face each contraction with resolve and control.

He followed her directions to the letter, gathering supplies and sterilizing them. More than once he wondered what he would have done for Debra if Brittany had not come to the island when she had. Wulff supposed that he would have managed to deliver the baby somehow, but he knew that he would never have been able to calmly encourage and coach the frightened girl the way this kind and gentle woman was doing.

Wulff knew that Brittany was anxious and concerned; anyone would be under the circumstances. But no trace of apprehension showed through the professional facade that she wore, a mask still thin enough to allow her compassion and empathy to show through.

"They're getting a lot stronger now, aren't they, honey?" she asked the girl.

Debra nodded.

"That's good. It won't be long now. I'm going to go scrub my hands."

Brittany left the room and returned several minutes later to find Wulff leaning over Debra, holding her hands.

"She just had two strong ones in a row," he said anxiously.

"Yes, that's normal at this point. Now comes the hard work, Debra," she said, "but your baby's almost here. Wulff, help me move her down toward the foot of the bed.

"There, that's good. Now you get up here by her head. When she has her next contraction, I want you to lift her shoulders and head like this. It'll make it easier for her to push. Okay?"

"Got it," he said, getting into position.

"I'm starting another one," the girl gasped.

"You can bear down now, Debra," she said. "Take a deep breath and push as hard as you can."

Wulff lifted the girl's shoulders, and she did as she was told.

"That's it. You're doing great. Hold your breath and keep pushing. Okay, that one's over. Rest and wait for the next contraction."

Wulff lowered the girl back onto the bed and smoothed her hair away from her flushed face. "How are you doin', Red? Are you okay?"

"Yes," she replied weakly, "I just hope it's over soon."

"It will be, sweetheart." He looked questioningly at Brittany. She nodded.

Through the next four contractions Debra pushed harder than any patient Brittany had ever seen.

At the peak of one of the hardest ones, she let out a yell, more from the extreme effort than from pain. Instantly they heard a knock on the bedroom door and a tearful, childish voice say, "Deb? Debbie? Are you dying?"

"She's all right, mate," Wulff shouted. "The baby's almost here. You run along now."

Three strong attempts produced the baby's head. Brittany quickly ran her finger around its neck.

"Wait, hold it! Wulff, don't let her push."

"Stop pushing, girl. Just breathe. What is it?"

"The cord's around the baby's neck. If she forces it now, the baby can strangle. Here, I'll have it off in a second."

Brittany quickly pulled the cord over the baby's head and away from its tiny neck.

"Okay. Go for it."

With one final effort Debra delivered the squirming infant into Brittany's waiting hands. It gasped and sputtered for breath, then delivered a gargled but lusty cry.

"Here you go, Debra." She held the baby up for their inspection. "It's a boy, a beautiful little nephew for Jesse." Then she carefully laid him on the girl's chest.

"Oh, just look at him, Mr. Wulff. Isn't he cute!" Debra cooed as she gingerly touched the baby's tiny shriveled fist.

"He sure is, Deb. He's wonderful." Wulff ran one rough finger along the infant's pink cheek. "I'm proud of you both," he added.

Brittany blinked back a tear or two. Darn, she always did that. No matter how many births she had witnessed, there was something about it that never failed to bring a tear to her eye.

She felt better when she saw Wulff blink rapidly a couple of times. Apparently he suffered the same weakness.

Murmuring that Debra needed some rest, Brittany picked up the baby again and gently wrapped him in a heavy, soft towel.

She handed the baby to Wulff. "Here, why don't you go introduce this young fellow to his anxious uncle?"

Wulff took the tiny bundle into his huge hands and carefully planted a kiss on its wrinkled forehead. "Well, what d'ya say, matie? Now we've got another dirty little bilge rat to throw overboard."

"You don't go throwing him anywhere for a while yet," Debra called after him as he left the room with his precious burden.

The girl slipped her hand into Brittany's and said, "I love Mr. Wulff. He's been so good to me and Jesse. And now I love you, too, Miss Davis. Thank you for helping me and my baby."

"You're welcome, sweetheart," Brittany said as she patted the freckled hand. "It's the best nursing I've ever done. I wouldn't have missed it for the world."

"I should have stayed." Brittany collapsed into the comfort of the light keeper's sofa.

"We've been through all of this before," Wulff said, sighing as he sank down next to her. "Where would you have slept? All they have is that one double bed for Debra and Grandma, and Jesse sleeps on the couch.

They don't even have a bathtub, for pete's sake. Were you going to sleep in the shower stall?''

"I should have stayed in my cabin. It couldn't have been as bad as you said.''

Wulff lifted his foot and showed her a damp deck shoe. He pointed to the darkened last few inches of his jeans.

"I'm telling you, it's flooded. I had to wade through five inches of water to get that lamp for you. It happens once or twice a year when there's a high tide and heavy winds. That cabin's too close to the beach.''

Wulff reached over and captured her hand in his. "Relax, Nurse Brittany. You said yourself that it was a perfectly normal delivery. They'll be fine.''

She slipped off her shoes and flexed her tired feet. "I know. It's just that, well, they're special. I've never had a patient that was all my own. I have to admit that I rather liked it. I liked it a lot.''

Reaching down he pulled her feet onto his lap. His thumbs gently massaged her arches, soothing, caressing. His fingers circled her ankles and worked their magic, imparting a tingling warmth that spread deliciously up her calves and thighs.

Brittany closed her eyes and sighed with pleasure. "Ah, that's wonderful.''

"You're wonderful,'' he replied softly.

She opened her eyes and found him watching her. His expressive eyes were shining with affection and something new—respect.

"That was a fine thing you did tonight, Nurse Brittany,'' he said. "A hell of a fine thing. You're a good woman.''

She smiled wearily. "Thank you. But what I am is a tired woman. Right now all I want out of life is a warm shower and a bed."

"Then you've got it. The bathroom is up the stairs, first door on the left." He rose and helped her to her feet. "I'm going to run up to the light and tell Bob he can go see his new cousin now that the wind's died down. Enjoy your shower."

"I will, believe me," she muttered, dragging her aching limbs up the stairs.

Brittany allowed the warm water to beat on the tense muscles of her neck. She knew that she shouldn't grant herself the luxury; on this island everyone conserved water. But she felt as though she deserved it this once.

The aching fatigue in her body gradually melted away, to be replaced by a glowing, euphoric contentment.

What could be more fulfilling than to bring a tiny person into the world, to feel him squirm with life in your hands and hear his first cries?

There was also the deep satisfaction of knowing that she had saved the child's life. A layman might not have discovered the cord around his neck until it was too late. Brittany couldn't bear the thought of Debra losing her baby. She and Jesse would be devastated.

Brittany smiled to herself as she stepped out of the shower and leisurely dried off with one of Wulff's fluffy brown towels. Yes, she was satisfied; it was a job well done.

Looking down at the pile of clothes that she had peeled off onto the floor, something inside her rebelled at the thought of putting them back onto her clean, refreshed body. She spotted Wulff's navy-blue, velour robe hanging on the back of the door, wondered if he would mind and then slipped into it.

The sleeves dangled nearly to her knees, and the hem dragged on the floor. She rolled up the cuffs until she could see her fingertips, and tied the belt tightly around her waist.

The masculine scent of his cologne and body lingered in the soft pile of the fabric. She breathed it in, feeling surrounded and caressed by the essence of the man.

Removing the towel that she had wrapped around her hair to keep it dry, she shook the golden tresses around her shoulders and noted with dismay that they were a mass of tangles.

The joys of motorcycle riding in a high wind, she thought as she picked up a brush from the bathroom counter and started back downstairs.

She found Wulff in the living room, lounging on the sofa, sipping from a mug of tea. On the chest sat a dainty porcelain cup with wisps of steam curling from its brim.

He laughed outright when he saw her shuffling along in the robe that engulfed her small frame.

"I hope you don't mind," she said.

"Not at all. I'll take you along the next time I go camping on Grand Bahama and stake you out for a tent. Here, I thought you might like something warm to drink before you hit the sack."

"Yes, thank you." Brittany sat on the couch, sipped the rich, strong liquid and found it too hot to drink. She placed the cup back on its saucer and began to brush her hair.

He watched her closely over the rim of his mug. "Feel better now?" he asked.

"Yes, much better. It's been a long day. I won't need anyone to rock me to sleep tonight."

"That's too bad," he murmured, watching the brush glide through the silken strands that glittered like finely polished brass in the lamplight.

Wulff set his mug beside her cup on the chest and held out his hand. "Would you mind?" he asked tentatively. "May I do that?"

She looked surprised, then quietly said, "Sure," and handed him the brush.

Turning her back to him, she folded her arms across the back of the sofa and buried her face in the crook of her elbow.

Wulff moved closer to her and began to slowly brush the mass of glossy curls. His featherlike strokes sent delightful, relaxing shivers throughout her body.

Patiently he worked until he had removed the last tangle, and the brush glided smoothly through the length without interference. Then he laid the brush aside and gathered the honey-colored tresses into his hands, running his fingers along the nape of her neck.

"Beautiful," he whispered, "absolutely beautiful."

He bent forward, and she thought for a moment that he was going to wrap his arms around her or kiss the back of her neck. At least she hoped so.

Instead he withdrew his hands, cleared his throat and said, "I think I need some more tea. How about you?"

Brittany lifted her face from her arms. "No, no thanks."

Wulff abruptly left the room and hurried into the kitchen. He poured his cold tea into the sink and reached for the teakettle on the stove. His hand was shaking with a tremor that was more than simple fatigue.

"Damn," he swore under his breath as he nearly dropped the steaming kettle. I can't go on like this, he thought desperately. I've never wanted or needed anyone half as much as I need that girl.

The word "girl" jarred his mind the second he thought it. He remembered the way Brittany had looked while soothing Debra, instructing him and tending the baby.

Wulff knew that after tonight he would never think of Brittany Davis as a girl again. She was a woman: a warm, intelligent, sensual woman.

Closing his eyes he leaned against the counter. His fingers gripped the edge for support as the realization overwhelmed him. It wasn't her innocence that he had been so zealously guarding. It was his own heart, his heart that had loved and lost more times than he could bear to recall.

He remembered his parents, his aunt, Michael and a young woman on Andros who had proved untrue. Like Brittany, everyone he had ever loved had died or walked out of his life. Her losses had caused her to open her heart and reach out to him. His had caused him to withdraw, closing himself off from the rest of the world here in this lonely, solitary place.

He smiled when he thought of how she had invaded his sanctuary, filling it with the sunlight of her golden hair and eyes. She had stirred those youthful desires that he had tried so hard to bury and forget. With her encouragement he had dared to dream again. She had made him love her, want her. And he did, desperately.

Turning off the flame under the teakettle, he walked back into the living room. He sighed and smiled when he saw her, stretched out, facedown on his couch. She was sound asleep. One arm dangled to the floor, her fingertips peeking from beneath the huge rolled cuff of his robe.

Her lovely hair lay spread across her back and face. She looked like an angel, a very tired angel. Wulff felt his lust subside as a tender, quieter emotion took its place.

Pulling a blanket from the old mahogany cupboard, he walked over to her. Carefully he brushed the hair away from her face and lifted her arm onto the sofa beside her.

He covered her with the blanket, tucking it around her sides and feet.

Then Wulff allowed himself one small kiss on her cheek before he turned out the lamp and went upstairs to bed.

Chapter Eight

Gentle, callused fingers reached from behind her and gathered her hair, pulling it away from the nape of her neck. She shivered as warm, moist lips tasted the delicate flavor of the skin on her shoulder.

Brittany felt his arms, heavily muscled arms, steal around her waist, gathering her to him. She allowed herself to lean back against him, delighting in the warmth and strength of his body as it molded itself to hers.

She didn't need to turn around because she knew who held her. She knew his touch, his scent, the masculine contours of his form.

"Wulff," she murmured, "I love you."

"I love you, too, Brittany," whispered the deep voice behind her.

"Then show me." She turned in his arms and looked into the depths of his pale blue eyes. Her hand slipped inside his shirt and stroked the soft mat of hair on his chest.

"Show me," she repeated.

Lifting her lips to his, she closed her eyes and waited in breathless anticipation for his kiss, the kiss that never came.

In the distance she could hear a bell, a ship's bell, chiming out the hour. Slowly she opened her eyes. Wulff was gone. Never in her life had Brittany Davis felt so empty and completely alone.

She stared into the darkness and wondered where she was. In the corner of the room a bit of brass gleamed in the silver moonlight, and she realized that it was a ship's clock that had awakened her.

A dream. She moaned and buried her face in the cushion of the sofa. It had only been a dream.

Her hand trailed down to the blanket that was spread over her. She didn't remember covering herself. The last thing she remembered was Wulff brushing her hair and—

Wulff. He had covered her and put out the light. But where was he now?

Her blood was still warm from the thrill of his touch, even if it had been only a dream. She wanted him. She wanted more than a caress in a midnight fantasy, and she didn't want to wait until morning.

Brittany left the sofa and blanket and felt her way across the dark room to the staircase. Carefully she climbed to the top of the steps and tiptoed down the narrow hallway. Passing the bathroom, she paused before a door that stood ajar at the end of the hall.

She took a deep breath and slowly pushed the door open.

The room was bathed in moonlight that streamed in through an open window to her left. The balmy night air bore the distant sounds of the waves on the rocks. Moonbeams cut a silver path across a large double bed. Directly in that path lay Wulff, his broad back and shoulders glistening in the pale light, his head and lower body in shadow.

Quietly she walked into the room and stopped beside the bed.

"Wulff?" she whispered softly.

He shifted and rolled onto his side. "Yes, love?"

"Are . . . are you asleep?"

"No, love. What is it?"

Brittany stood gazing at his muscular torso that gleamed like Michelangelo's David in the moonlight. She wished that she could see his face, his eyes.

"I miss you," she murmured softly. "I want to...be with you."

He raised himself onto one elbow and was silent for what seemed like an eternity.

Then he said, "Are you sure, Brittany? Be sure, because I'm only going to give you this one chance to change your mind."

Her hands moved to the bathrobe belt tied at her waist. "A chance to change my mind isn't what I want from you, Wulff."

Slowly she untied the belt, then stepped into the path of the moonlight. "That isn't what I want from you at all."

The only sounds were those of the sea and of his sharp intake of breath as she slowly opened the robe and slipped it off her shoulders. It fell away from her body into a soft heap on the floor.

She stood still, allowing the moon to bathe her nakedness with its silvery light. A wave of self-consciousness swept over her, making her want to reach down and retrieve the robe that she had carelessly cast aside.

Wulff slowly sat up in his bed. The sheet that had covered him to the waist, fell low around his hips. When his face moved into the light, her embarrassment vanished. The wonder in his eyes as he gazed at her body made her feel beautiful and completely feminine in a way that she had never felt before.

"My God," he whispered reverently. "I'll never forget the way you look right now. You're the loveliest sight I've ever seen."

"Then tell me you love me, Wulff. Tell me you want me."

He held out his arms to her. She could see the wolf's head glowing on his rounded biceps. "I love you, sweetheart, and I want you. Come here and I'll show you how much."

She moved closer to the bed and put her hands in his. He quickly pulled her down to sit beside him.

One big hand cupped her chin as he turned her face into the moonlight and looked lovingly into her eyes. "I was just lying here, thinking how much I want to touch you . . . and kiss you."

His lips brushed her forehead and eyelids with feathery kisses. "Thank you for coming to me," he murmured, his voice husky with emotion.

She allowed her palm to glide over the rounded muscles of his chest, down to the side of his hip, bared by the fallen sheet. "I had to come. I love you." Her voice trembled as she whispered, "Wulff, make love to me, please."

His fingertips trailed down her throat and slowly brushed away the golden cascade that covered her breasts, exposing their delicate beauty to the moonlight and his gaze.

"Oh, I will, sweetheart," he said as he drew her down onto the bed beside him. "I most certainly will."

Brittany shivered with delight as the length of her naked body met his for the first time between the crisp sheets. She basked in the warmth that radiated from him as he wrapped his arms and legs over her, enveloping her in a cloak of love.

His lips descended on hers in a long, luxurious kiss of tenderness and affection. His tongue lightly teased the corners of her mouth, coaxing her lips to part and allow him inside.

As his tongue leisurely explored the moist softness of her mouth, his hands traveled over her body, memorizing every velvety contour.

She quivered with feverish excitement as his rough fingers circled her breast, nearly but not quite brushing the taut, inflamed nipple that longed for his touch.

Eagerly she covered his hand with hers and moved it toward the aching, rosy tip.

He chuckled deep in his throat and sighed. "Ah...the impatience of youth."

"Yes, I'm impatient," she admitted breathlessly. "Aren't you?"

"No."

Slowly, deliberately, he kneaded the creamy softness in his hand, while his lips caressed a sensitive spot on her neck below her ear. "For years I've waited for you, Brittany. All my life I've held the dream of you here in my heart. Now that I can actually hold you in my arms, I'm going to enjoy this and make it last as long as I can.''

His lips blazed a burning path down her throat to her breast. "I want to know you before I take you, love," he whispered. "I want to know every soft, sweet inch of you. So just lie back and enjoy it. There's no hurry. We have all night.''

His mouth moved over her white flesh, burning it with its warm, wet heat. His tongue circled her nipple, then flicked it teasingly until she writhed below him in sweet agony.

Lifting her head, she buried her face and hands in his thick mane and clutched him to her chest. When she thought she would die of anticipation, he answered her burning desire by opening his mouth and taking in as much of her breast as he could.

She could feel the long, hard length of his body tense with rising passion.

He devoured first one breast and then the other until their urgent needs were fully satisfied.

But there were other desires blossoming in her body, other parts that burned for his touch. His hand moved lower, down her abdomen to her inner thigh where, for what seemed an eternity, he circled, drawing close to the center of her femininity, then pulling away to begin its circuit toward her inner knee.

"Wulff, you're making me crazy. Please..."

He laughed softly. "Please what? Tell me what you want.''

"Oh God, you know what I want. Touch me, please.''

"Where?" he whispered wickedly. "Where do you want me to touch you, love?" His hand trailed up her thigh with agonizing slowness.

She shuddered violently as it neared its goal.

He gently nudged her thighs apart and began a slow, but thorough, sensual exploration. "Here? Is this what you had in mind?" he asked as he gently probed the depths of her sexuality.

A low moan escaped her lips as she arched shamelessly to meet his hand.

"Yes," he said softly, "I thought that's what you meant."

Brittany surrendered herself to his skillful attention, reveling in the glorious sensations he aroused.

Slowly his lips and tongue traced a path of kisses over her breasts and down her midriff; a warm, moist trail dipped lower and lower, stirring waves of ecstasy that rippled through her, leaving her weak and trembling.

Wulff had meant what he had said; he wanted to know her completely, and he did. Slowly he savored the sweetness of her body's desire, as she quivered and moaned with pleasure.

"Oh, Aren," she gasped, "I can't stand much more of this."

"Neither can I," he replied, his breath coming in ragged gasps. His lips and tongue retraced the trail back up her body. But this time the slow, teasing lethargy had disappeared, and his mouth consumed her with an ever-increasing urgency.

As his lips once again took hers, Brittany ran her hands down his hard, lean body until her fingers closed around his throbbing shaft. At her touch the giant body beside her shuddered, and she heard him groan as she had done moments before.

Then he was moving over her, and in a moment his body had found and united with hers. Slowly, carefully he entered her, filling her with more pleasure than she had ever thought she could hold.

His first strokes were short and quick, causing her to writhe beneath him in exquisite frustration. She wrapped her legs tightly around his waist and arched her body so that he could penetrate even more deeply.

His response was quick and strong. He drove into her with deep, hard thrusts that brought cries of pleasure from her as the burning tension in her body wound tighter and tighter.

Suddenly the fire inside her exploded, sending shooting sparks into every part of her body. The intensity of her climax overwhelmed her, and she gripped his shoulders, digging her fingertips into the hard, unyielding flesh.

The convulsing of her body beneath his sent him over the edge. With one final thrust, he plunged deeply into her, filling her with all of his pent-up desires and passions.

Moments later, they lay side by side, still intimately joined. She offered her lips to him and he kissed them softly, tenderly.

"I've never... I mean, it's never been that way for me before," she stammered.

"Yes, I know," he replied, kissing her again. "Me either."

"Really?" she asked.

"Yes, really. Thank you." He tenderly brushed a wisp of hair from her face and kissed her cheek. "Ah, Brittany, after all these years I've finally found you," he murmured, pulling her close to his heart. "You were a dream that was well worth waiting for."

* * *

Wulff laid his jeweler's rouge and cloth on the floor of the chamber and turned away from the lens. He'd been polishing for more than an hour, and it was time for a break. Besides, he couldn't keep his mind on his work anyway.

Every time he thought of her, of the way she had been in his arms, a heavy warmth settled in his loins, making him want her again.

He had wakened at dawn and watched her as she slept, her long lashes brushing her cheeks, her golden hair spread across his pillow.

It had been the first time in Wulff's life that he had opened his eyes to find another person lying beside him. And he knew that he never wanted to start another day without her.

It had been difficult letting her go that morning, even though he had known that it would only be for a few hours. She had been so anxious to get down the hill and see how Debra and the baby were doing.

Delivering Debra's baby had been the best thing that could have happened to Brittany. She seemed so much happier and stronger. Having someone to care for was what she had needed to jar her out of her depression over Michael's death.

Michael. Wulff felt a sharp pang of guilt and anxiety. If he truly cared about Brittany and what was best for her, he would have gotten her off the island one way or another, at least for the next couple of weeks.

But after the previous night, he knew that she wouldn't leave, and that he could never force her. He'd have to be very careful and keep an eye on her. He couldn't bear the thought of her being hurt, and she certainly would be if she got involved.... He'd have to make sure that she didn't.

Wulff walked out onto the balcony and looked down at the jagged rocks of the cove. Michael, you damned fool, he thought.

Then he saw her, a slender figure in jean shorts and a yellow T-shirt, climbing over the rocks, heading down to the cove.

So, she had decided to come back via the scenic route. Even from a distance he could see the delicate contours of her body beneath the thin fabric of her shirt. The heaviness began to build again as he remembered the incredible softness of those curves.

He watched as she ran to the water's edge, playfully scooped a handful of foam and threw it at a gull that circled her head. She was in a lighthearted mood. Apparently things had been good with Debra and her baby.

Wulff's brow furrowed as he watched her walk to the boat house and disappear inside. His frown deepened when she reappeared with a flashlight in her hand.

"Damn," he muttered as she went into the largest cave. "Bloody damn."

The light keeper hesitated, his mind churning. He had to do something, but what? He couldn't let her mess with those rocks. But how could he stop her without making her even more curious than she already was?

A slow, mischievous smile curled his lips. He knew how to distract Nurse Brittany. Yes, indeed.

"What do you think you're doing?" boomed a deep voice from out of the darkness of the cave.

Brittany jumped to her feet and nearly dropped her flashlight. She placed one hand over her heart and gasped. "My God, Wulff, you scared me half to death."

"And well you should be scared, wench. Do you know whose cave this is that you're poking about in? And whose treasure lies buried within yonder stones?"

Wulff shifted the beach towel that he held under his arm and shone his light into her eyes. They sparkled playfully, glinting like twenty-four-carat gold.

"Let me guess," she said, walking away from the rocks that she had been examining. "A band of fierce pirates. Maybe even Long John Silver?"

"Nay, Johnny's a wimp compared to the band of ruffians that inhabit this cave."

"Of whom I suppose you are the captain?"

He grinned broadly. "Of course." Dropping his light, he quickly crossed the short distance between them and grasped her firmly around the waist.

"Too bad for you, wench, that you've fallen into my clutches."

Brittany twined her arms around his neck. "Um... yeah...that's too bad." She stood on tiptoe and lightly kissed his chin. "But whatever will you do to me now that you have me, sir?" she asked in her best Southern drawl.

Wulff pulled the beach towel from under his arm, unrolled it and spread it on the floor of the cave. Then, he grasped her around the waist and lowered her onto the soft terry cloth. Lying beside her, he draped one heavy, solid thigh across her lower body and pinned her to the ground.

He raised her hands above her head, holding them easily with one hand. With the other he picked up the flashlight that she had dropped and shone it into her face.

"What am I going to do to you? Aye, that is a problem. What shall we do with the lass now that we've got her, mates? Shall we make 'er walk the plank?"

"Nay," she protested, struggling beneath him. "The plank's broken, remember?"

"Aye, that's right. I keep forgettin'. Gotta get that darned thing fixed. Perhaps we should throw her overboard. Would serve her right, trying to steal our treasure like that. Yeah, we'll pitch her overboard."

"Nay, sir, not that."

"Well, why not?"

"Begging the captain's pardon, sir," she said, batting her thick lashes, "but there are other uses for a wench."

"Aye, that's right. 'Tis the fate worse than death you mean. It would be a waste to throw such a tasty morsel to the sharks."

He laid the flashlight aside and ran his hand lightly down the front of her T-shirt, pausing to caress her breasts. "'Tis a winsome wench we have here, lads. She even has her own treasure chest."

"Oh, God," Brittany moaned and then giggled. "Ravish me if you must, cruel sir, but spare me the awful puns."

"All right," he growled, "you've had it now. And to think that I was going to be gentle with you out of respect for your virginity."

"My virginity?"

"Well, I was going to give you the benefit of the doubt in spite of those rumors about your wanton conduct with a certain lighthouse keeper."

"Lies, sir," she protested, "all lies. I'm as pure as the driven slush."

"Oh, yeah? Well, not for long. Evil deeds such as these should be cloaked in darkness."

He reached over and switched off the flashlight. They were plunged into a velvet blackness, void of sight, but rich in the other senses.

Wulff's soft breath fanned her cheek as he lowered his face to hers. "Be mine, fair maiden, surrender your charms to me."

"Never," she vowed, her voice echoing in the darkness. "This time, Captain Wulff, if you'll be getting any satisfaction from me, you'll pay the price."

She heard a deep growl before his warm mouth sought and found hers. He kissed her roughly, plundering her lips and invading her soft recesses until he felt the sharp edge of her teeth on his tongue. It was a gentle enough nip, yet sharp enough to cause him to withdraw and find a safer place to ravish.

"So, 'tis a fight you want, eh?" he murmured, tasting the delicate flavor of a pulse spot on her neck. "'Tis nothing a scoundrel like meself likes better than a tussle with a lusty lass."

Wulff felt her warm, sensuous body squirm beneath him and chuckled at her mock cries of protest as he slipped his hand beneath the soft fabric of her T-shirt.

He reached behind her, lifted her slightly and unclasped her bra. His hand slid around to cup the exquisite softness he had released.

Brittany twisted, reveling in her delicious helplessness. In glorious surrender she arched her body against his as he ravenously devoured the treasures he had uncovered.

As his mouth took her breasts, his hand moved over her quivering abdomen to the waistband of her shorts. In the darkness he groped for the button and found it, twisting it open with his fingers. With one quick jerk he had pulled the zipper down, leaving the satin of her panties exposed to his searching fingers.

"No, please," she cried, wriggling beneath the hard swell of his thigh. "I'm saving myself for another."

"Who?" he asked, peeling the shorts away from her hips.

"The keeper of Wolf Light."

"Oh, don't worry about him. I'll trade him a case of fine Caribbean rum and ten shillings for your charms."

His hand slid inside the satin and explored the moist softness there. "Ah, make that two cases of rum and twenty shillings, and 'tis a bargain at that."

He stripped away the bit of satin and nudged her thighs apart. "Now here...here is treasure worth finding."

Her argument was diluted by moans and gasps of delight as his fingers gently prodded and caressed her into a frenzy of desire.

Wulff shifted and sat astride her hips, not putting his whole weight on her, but enough to keep her effectively trapped beneath him. Then he released her hands, and she heard him pull his shirt over his head and toss it aside.

Her freed hands reached out in the darkness and found the rounded muscles and thick hair of his chest. She glided her palms over his skin, savoring the fine mist of sweat that their vigorous play had evoked.

Her fingers sought the snap of his jeans. She eagerly lowered the zipper and reached inside his briefs. Her hand closed over a turgid swelling, something else that their game had produced.

Wulff moaned and grasped her breasts, stroking them with the same rhythm that she stroked him.

"An eager lass, aren't you?"

"Yes," she gasped.

"Are you about ready to relinquish that precious virtue of yours?"

"Yes, yes, take it."

Wulff laughed heartily and moved into position between her thighs. He cupped her hips with his hands and lifted her body to meet his.

With one sharp, stabbing thrust he entered her, plunging into her honeyed sweetness. Again and again he drove into her, possessing her as she surrendered fully to him.

Playful games were forgotten as Brittany felt herself lost in the darkness that swirled around her, lost in the waves of sensation that began in the depths of her being and rolled outward to engulf her limbs in their wake.

Wulff felt her shudder beneath him and heard her cry out his name until it echoed over and over against the walls around them.

Her body gripped him, squeezed him until at last his own passion exploded inside her and filled her to overflowing.

The erotic scents of their lovemaking mingled with the musty smell of the cave as they settled into each other's arms, basking in the afterglow of loving.

They lay side by side on the towel for a long time afterward, whispering the tender words of fulfilled lovers. The cool, damp air of the cave made the heat of their bodies even warmer, more delicious to the other.

Finally they gathered their clothes in the darkness and helped each other dress.

"So, am I to expect this kind of abuse every time I enter your cave, Captain Wulff?" she asked as he helped her fasten her bra.

"Every time," he threatened.

"Oh, good. Then I'll meet you here tomorrow."

Wulff sighed and zipped his jeans. So much for bright ideas, he thought, and so much for keeping Nurse Brittany out of the caves.

Chapter Nine

Wulff, put me down. Put me down this instant."

"Or you'll do what?" he asked as he hoisted her even higher on his shoulder and carried her out of the darkness of the cave into the bright sunlight.

From where she hung, head down, facing his back, it was difficult to deliver any convincing, violent threats.

"I won't play 'walk the plank' with you anymore," she offered lamely.

"Then maybe I should pitch you overboard after all and be done with you."

"No!" she screamed as he carried her toward the water. "Wulff, don't you dare. I don't have any dry clothes. Don't, no!"

He pulled her from his shoulder, and with one arm around her waist dangled her over the foaming waves.

"So, you're going to hold out on me, huh? No more fooling around, huh?"

He swung her farther out over the water.

"I was kidding, really. Anything you say. But don't drop me."

Wulff laughed and slowly lowered her to her feet on dry sand. "Well, hell, you're no fun," he said, pushing back the hair that had fallen across her face. "Jesse lets me throw him in."

"I'm no fun? Mister, you've got a lot of nerve to tell me that I'm no fun after what we just did."

"That's true. I take it all back." He gathered her close to him, his hands caressing the rounded softness of her hips.

"In fact, you're more fun than—"

The words froze in his mouth, and Brittany looked up to see his icy stare fixed upon something behind her.

She turned in his arms to see what had caused his reaction. Coming down the beach toward them was the fat man who had been with Aren the day before in the cove. His eyes matched Wulff's, cold and forbidding.

Apparently he had arrived while they were in the cave. His ugly green boat was docked at the boat house.

She felt Aren's hands tighten on her shoulders as the man drew nearer. He pulled her protectively to his side.

"Hello, Wulff. Nice day," the man mumbled when he reached them. His tone was much less cordial than his greeting. "And who's this?" His lecherous gaze swept Brittany from head to toe.

"This is a friend of mine," Wulff replied guardedly, drawing her even closer.

"I'm Jack Evans," the man said, holding out a beefy, chafed hand to her. "And who might you be, pretty lady?"

Brittany ignored the outstretched hand. Something about the sleazy way his eyes moved over her, combined with the puffy, unhealthy look of his skin, made her reluctant to touch him.

"I'm Brittany Davis," she replied.

"Davis?" he asked. His watery eyes darted back to the keeper.

"That's right," Wulff snapped. "Like I said, she's a friend of mine."

Evans shuffled his feet awkwardly and shoved his hands into his pockets. Brittany felt a cold chill as his plaid jacket gaped open and revealed the thin, leather strap of a shoulder holster. She glanced quickly away and saw Wulff's eyes on her.

"Jack and I have some...business to discuss," he told her. "Would you mind waiting for me in the house? It won't take long."

She glanced from Wulff to Evans, who seemed to have an unwholesome interest in the Community Hospital logo on the front of her T-shirt.

"Sure, no problem." Turning on her heel Brittany started up the path toward the house. As she walked away she heard Evans say in a conspiratorial tone, "You said you'd be alone today."

"So, I got lucky," Wulff snapped impatiently. "Don't worry about the girl. She's my problem."

What? Brittany whirled around to face Wulff. Got lucky? Surely he hadn't said that—

The movement of her turning caught Wulff's eye. One look into her stricken face told him that she had overheard his statement.

He muttered a curse and started up the hill toward her. Then he hesitated and turned back to Evans, who seemed to be enjoying the scene with sadistic humor.

Damn him, she thought. Damn them both. She turned and strode up the hill. A constriction tightened her throat, forcing tears to her eyes. Angrily she blinked them away.

She could feel their eyes burning her back as she stumbled clumsily up the rock-strewn path. Slowing her pace, she straightened her spine and tried to summon some degree of dignity.

At the top of the path she turned to look back at them. Their heads were bent low, and they appeared to be arguing about something.

Brittany hesitated at the base of the light. She rebelled against the idea of being told what to do, and refused to go to the house as Aren had asked. She would wait all right, but she would wait wherever she damn well pleased.

She pulled open the heavy steel door and entered the tower. Climbing the spiraling staircase, she knew that she had come into the lighthouse for a more practical reason than a simple act of rebellion. She wanted to be able to keep an eye on the two men without them knowing it, and what better place was there to do that?

When Brittany reached the top of the stairs, she stayed in the lantern chamber rather than go out on the balcony and risk being seen. Standing on her tiptoes, she could barely see the men as they walked slowly up the path toward the base of the light. A moment later they disappeared from sight beneath the balcony, and she was left with her burning questions.

What kind of man was Evans that Aren changed in his presence? What business could a reputable light keeper have with a man who carried a gun? Why couldn't Wulff discuss it around the woman he loved?

The woman he loved? Did he love her? What kind of man makes passionate love to a woman and fifteen minutes later refers to her as a girl and a problem?

He had spoken of her as though she were an easy, meaningless conquest. No, she hadn't been a conquest. She hadn't even been a challenge.

Covering her face with both hands she tried to blot out the shame that flooded over her as she remembered how she had fallen into his arms on the balcony—how she had gone to his bed and begged him to make love to her.

Oh, God, why had she degraded herself that way? Why had she deceived herself into thinking that he actually loved her?

She stifled a sob as she heard the door at the base of the tower open and shut.

Male voices drifted up to her from below and she could clearly hear every word echoing through the tower.

"Davis's sister? Well, that's great. What the hell are you going to do about her?"

"I already told you," came Wulff's bass voice, "I've got her under control. She's not going to be a problem."

"And what if she finds out what really happened to her brother? Are you going to be able to handle her then?"

"She's not going to find out. She's staying here with me now, and I'm keeping an eye on her every minute."

Brittany clamped her hand over her mouth to muffle a gasp. Michael? My God, what about Michael? Her knees went weak and nearly buckled beneath her.

Evans continued, "You've got her staying here with you, huh? Now, isn't that cozy. I suppose you're taking full advantage of the opportunity, grieving sister and all that."

"Shut up, Evans. You're slime, you know that? I don't know why I waste my time on you."

"Because, you want him as much as I do. And we're going to get him, too. He'll be coming through Friday night, and this time it's going to work."

"Do you have the false light set up yet?" Wulff asked.

"It's taken care of. You worry about your end of it. Be ready to turn out that light at the right time."

Brittany's pounding heart leaped into her throat, suffocating her. She backed against the wall of the chamber for support. A false light? She thought of Captain Jonathan Wulff. The bitter taste of hate filled her mouth.

"I know my part in this," she heard Wulff say. "Lord knows, we've gone over it often enough. You better hope that there's fog Friday night. It'll have to be a heavy one, too, because there'll be a full moon."

"Oh, there'll be fog. We modern day wreckers have lots of advantages that the old fellows didn't have. All they had were rocks and clubs. We have weather reports and revolvers. Ah, the advances of technology."

"Get out of here, Evans. You're stinking up my light. And once this is over, you stay the hell away from Wolf Rock."

"When this is over, Wulff, I won't need you any-more. Then you and your damned lighthouse can go to blazes for all I care."

Brittany heard the door open and close again and the echo of footsteps on the iron staircase. She waited. Her body shook with rage and fear. Her pulse throbbed in her ears.

Wulff's head appeared at the top of the stairs. When he saw her standing there, his face went white beneath its tan.

"Brittany, I . . . I thought you were in the house."

"Obviously." Her eyes flashed golden fire.

Wulff slowly walked toward her, his face tight, his eyes searching hers.

"I don't know what you think you heard, but—"

"I heard it all, you bastard." Her chest heaved and hot tears stung her eyelids. "Did . . . did you kill my brother?"

His eyes softened and he reached one hand out to her. "No, love, of course not. Is that what you think?"

"Don't touch me!" she shouted, slapping his hand away. "I don't know what the hell I think right now. I heard you and that Evans creep planning to kill some-body. What am I supposed to think?"

"Brittany, honey." Wulff reached his hand out to her again, then let it drop to his side. "Trust me. I can explain all of that."

"Well, go ahead, explain it to me. I'm listening." Brittany could hear the desperation in her own voice, the feeble hope that somehow he would be able to jus-tify that which could not be justified.

Wulff hesitated, then sighed and ran his fingers through his hair. "I could, but I won't," he said. "I won't clear myself by hurting you. This mess is all my fault. I should have gotten you off the island when I had the chance.''

"Oh, that's all right, Aren," she replied with cutting sarcasm. "After all, you have this little problem under control, right?"

Wulff's face flushed scarlet. His temper flared. "Damn it, woman! I didn't mean that the way it sounded. I was trying to convince Evans that you weren't a threat. Believe me, I've had your best interests at heart—most of the time, at least."

"Well, don't bother yourself about my best interests, Aren. I told you before, I can take care of myself. Next time I'll know better than to fall in love with someone I hardly know."

Taking a wide circuit around him, she walked to the top of the stairs. She stopped, her hand gripping the rail, and said, "I loved you, Aren. I really did."

Scalding tears coursed down her cheeks. She could taste their bitter saltiness in the corners of her mouth.

She despised the trembling in her voice when she said, "I thought you were a good and decent man. How was I supposed to know that you're a damned moon curser, just like your great-grandfather?"

Wulff stood like a stone as her words gradually filtered into his brain. His jaw tightened and his eyes blazed. "What the hell are you talking about?"

"You know damned well what I'm talking about. After all, wrecking seems to be a part of your sacred family tradition."

He lowered his voice menacingly. "Look, I know you're upset right now and more than a little confused. But you'd better watch your mouth when you go making accusations about my family that you have no basis for."

"No basis?" Her anger threw all restraint to the wind. She wanted to hurt him, badly, like he had hurt her. "I have concrete proof. The only reason that I haven't shown it to you already is because I loved you, and I didn't want to destroy your pride in your family heritage. Now that's a joke, isn't it?"

"Well, if it is, it's a sick joke and I'm not laughing."

"Neither am I. I'm leaving." She started down the spiraling staircase.

Quickly he crossed the short space between them. "No you aren't. You're not going anywhere until you explain what you said."

"Oh, yeah?" She glared at him over her shoulder. "You just watch me."

"Brittany, for God's sake, wait a minute!" he shouted as he hurried down the stairs after her. "Listen to me, please. We both need time to cool off. But whatever you do, don't tell anyone what you heard here today. Please. There's more to this than I can tell you. And it's very important that you don't talk to anybody about it."

She reached the bottom of the stairs and paused before the steel door. "What's the matter, Wulff? Are you afraid that I'll report you to the authorities?"

"No, I'm afraid that you're going to get hurt, even more than you already are."

He walked over to where she stood by the door and cupped her face in his hands.

"Brittany, think about the way we were together last night. In spite of what you just heard, you and I were lovers, and that has to count for something."

His fingers gently stroked her fevered cheeks; his thumbs smoothed away her tears. "Can you trust me this once, just enough to do what I'm asking of you? Go back to the cabin, and don't say anything to anybody until you hear from me. Promise me that you'll do that, please."

She jerked her head away from his hands. Before she had craved his touch; now it made her feel sick inside.

"I don't know, Wulff. I can't promise you anything right now."

"I love you. I really do," he said before she left the tower, closing the door behind her.

His words echoed in her heart and mind all the way down the hill.

Brittany threw the mop to the floor of the cabin, fell onto the daybed and covered her head with a pillow.

Tidal waves of confusion swept over her, threatening to drag her into a sea of despair. She had never felt so completely at odds with herself and her feelings. She was experiencing a hundred different emotions, and all of them were contradictory.

More than anything in the world, she wanted to run back up to the light, fall into Wulff's strong arms and pour out her heart to him. She would tell him how confused and hurt she was, and he would hold her close and make her feel safe and secure.

But, of course, that was the one thing that she could never do. Wulff was a wrecker, a murderer, like his great-grandfather. Or at least, that was the only way that she could interpret the conversation she had overheard.

If he were truly innocent, why hadn't he explained himself to her when she had given him the chance? Because there was no explanation. There could be no justification for lighting a false light and luring a man through the fog to the rocks of the cove. A hundred years ago there had been no justification, and there was none now.

Besides, Wulff didn't really love her. He had only used her. No, it was worse than that. She had begged to be used, and he had accepted her offer.

And the worst thing of all was that if she didn't do something to stop them, Wulff and Evans were going to kill someone Friday night. They might have even killed Michael.

Yet, Brittany had believed Wulff when he said that he hadn't murdered her brother. There was a certain sincerity in his eyes that she didn't think he could fake.

But then, she had believed him when he had said that he loved her, too. Either way, she knew that there was more to Michael's death than he had told her.

Wulff was hiding so many things from her: his reason for wanting her to leave the island, his interest in the stones in the cave, the nature of his involvement with Evans, the circumstances surrounding Michael's death. Why would he keep these things from her if he were innocent? He wouldn't. He just wouldn't.

Brittany buried her face deeper into the pillow, seeking its comforting softness. Giant sobs racked her body as she gave in to the despair and depression that could no longer be held at bay.

For what seemed like an eternity, she allowed the emotions to wash through her like a cleansing flood.

When at last she lay completely spent, the only feeling left was fatigue, a total weariness of mind, body and spirit.

The sunlight that came through the windows of the cabin began to fade, and the shadows of the room deepened. She felt the veil of sleep settle over her, bringing its lulling anesthetic to her mind.

"Michael," she whispered, before her weighted eyelids closed. "Michael, how did you die? I'm so confused. Help me."

As she slept an unusually strong draft tenderly swept a lock of hair away from her tear-swollen face.

Moonlight, diffused by a light haze of fog, filtered through the tattered curtains of the seaside cottage. The silver globe cast its muted light on the bed, where the young woman tossed and turned fitfully.

Her slender fingers clutched the sheet that she had pulled around her shoulders, and her lips murmured the incoherent mutterings of a dreamer.

Behind her closed eyelids she saw a world where there was no moonlight, only raging, turbulent darkness.

Brittany stood at the water's edge on a black, sand swept, wind ravaged beach. The screaming gale threw a stinging, saline mixture of ocean spray and sand into her face. She covered her eyes with her hands, trying to shield them from the wind that moaned like a live thing in torment as it whipped her hair and the thin, white nightgown that she had clutched around her.

Exhausted from struggling to stay on her feet, she sank to her knees on the wet sand. With the back of her hand she wiped the brine from her eyes and lips and peered through the murky gloom into the heart of the cove, where billows surged and crashed against the rocks that jutted from its center.

She gasped as a dim outline began to take shape before her eyes. Against the blackness of the night the dark, ominous form of a ship materialized. The vessel's black masts and spars towered above her, supporting only the torn remnants of once proud sails.

The ship's groans mixed with those of the wind as the vessel struggled on rocks that gored her sides, splitting her hull. Her life's blood, her crew, spilled into the churning black waters around her, pitiful bits of humanity lost to the fury of the sea.

Some of them were tossed, screaming, against the razor-sharp, jagged rocks. Others disappeared into the blackness of the surging depths where their lifeless, waterlogged bodies were swept out to sea.

A few made it to the shore and lay facedown, bleeding and gasping for breath.

Brittany was overwhelmed with the horror of the scene. The relentless rage of the sea as it tore the life from the ship and its men was more than her mind could take in... a savage, mindless power that no one and nothing could withstand.

She struggled to her feet and turned her back on the scene. Part of her knew that she was dreaming and hoped that when she looked again, the cove would be filled with golden sunlight and swooping seabirds.

Then her eyes were drawn to a dark, cylindrical shape, which rose from the black outline of the hill above her. A lighthouse. Standing on the balcony was a man. In the darkness her heart told her what her eyes could not. He was the keeper of Wolf Light. And she knew that his pale blue eyes watched the horrors below even as she watched.

Something compelled her to draw her gaze from the man in the tower and turn back toward the cove.

That was when she saw him... a man, not six feet away, crawling toward her. A dark wound on the side of his head oozed blood, and one arm dangled uselessly by his side as he dragged his body across the sand.

She stood, frozen for a moment, then hurried to him. When she reached his side, he clutched at the hem of her long nightgown and uttered deep, guttural sounds of pain that were quickly carried away on the wind.

Dropping to her knees beside him, she cradled his injured head in her arms and covered the wound with her palm in a vain attempt to stanch the flow of blood that poured down his face and onto the sand.

Brittany bent her head close to his and tried to hear his garbled words. "My ship...Elizabeth," came the tortured gasp. "My men, please, help my men."

Brittany clutched the man even tighter in her arms as the stunning realization overwhelmed her.

"I'll try, Captain," she shouted above the storm. "I'll try to help them."

She closed her eyes and held him close, unwilling to let him go. She knew that he was dying and felt the overpowering need to hold him as long as she could.

But when she opened her eyes again, he had somehow changed. The man whom she now held in her arms was also injured. His blood stained her hand even as the captain's had and he, too, had the look of death about him.

Brittany felt her body shake violently and heard herself scream, a long scream of hysteria. Reaching down, she placed one hand on his blond hair and stared into the man's eyes that were already glazing over.

"No," she sobbed, trying once again to stop the flow of blood with her hand. "Michael, don't...don't leave me."

For an instant, she saw a flicker of recognition in his eyes. "Susie," he whispered hoarsely, his breath rattling in his throat. Then his glazed eyes focused on something over her shoulder.

Brittany turned her head and looked behind her. Out of the murky blackness loomed the form of a man. As he came nearer she saw that he was looking right through her as though she weren't there. His eyes were riveted on the man who lay on the sand. In his hand he held a large stone.

His face was somehow familiar to her, but his features were distorted with fear and indecision. A look of dark resolution settled on his face as he raised the rock over his head.

Brittany tried to throw herself between the man and her brother, but her limbs were weighted with that unique paralysis that is reserved for tormented dreamers.

"No!" she screamed. "No!"

A split second later, the rock descended. Her brother's skull was crushed beneath the shattering blow.

Chapter Ten

Dawn had barely broken when Brittany was awakened by a gentle rap at the door. With her heart
pounding she crawled out of bed and answered the
knock, which was growing more insistent by the moment.

She opened the door a crack and saw Wulff filling
the doorway. His hair was uncombed, and a rough
stubble of beard covered his chin and cheeks. He wore
the same blue T-shirt and faded jeans that he had worn
the day before. His clothes looked as though he had
slept in them, but his face looked as though he hadn't
slept in days.

She felt a fleeting surge of joy at seeing him. Even in
his disheveled state he was the most handsome man she
had ever seen. And he had come to her, first thing in
the morning. Brittany quickly pushed the feeling aside
as her suspicions and doubts reasserted themselves.

They stared into each other's eyes for several moments before either of them spoke. Finally Wulff broke the silence.

"I'm ready," he said simply.

"Ready to do what?" she asked.

He drew a deep breath and sighed. "I'm ready to tell you anything that you want to know. I thought about it all night—" His voice broke and he swallowed hard.

With one hand he pushed the door open and walked inside. Brittany stepped back, feeling her heart lurch at his nearness. She turned away from him and walked to the window, unwilling for him to see the tears that she had tried to blink away.

Wulff crossed the room and stood quietly behind her. His hand trailed lightly down the back of her hair.

"I can imagine what you must be thinking and feeling," he said, his voice thick with emotion. "Believe me, I imagined it all night—and about went crazy."

His fingers slipped beneath her hair and delicately massaged the back of her neck. "I should have explained it all to you yesterday in the lighthouse. But I love you and I couldn't bear to hurt you. You've been through so much already."

She whirled to face him, no longer caring if he saw the tears that rained down her cheeks. "And you don't think I'm hurting now? What could you possibly say that could make me feel any worse than I already feel?"

"Brittany, sweetheart, I'm so sorry." He brushed her tears away with his fingertips, wrapped his arms around her waist and pulled her against him.

The scent and warmth of his body filled her senses as his big hands softly caressed her back. It would be so easy to melt against him, to let go and . . .

"No, Wulff, please," she pleaded.

"What, love? What can I do to make it better?"

Her eyes trailed down his face to his lips, so full, so sensuous—and only inches away from hers.

"Leave. Please, just leave."

He pulled back and searched her eyes. She thought she saw a trace of anger cross his features.

"Okay, I'll leave if that's what you want. I'll walk out of your life, and you won't ever have to see me again. But first I want you to look me in the eye, and tell me that you weren't happy to see me when you opened that door a minute ago. I want you to tell me that you don't love me anymore."

His eyes lowered to watch her trembling lower lip. "And that you don't want me to kiss you right now," he added.

Brittany gulped and closed her eyes. She couldn't tell him anything. She couldn't speak. She couldn't even look at him.

His lips touched hers, gently, tenderly. She heard herself whimper and felt her hands seeking his hair. Her fingers twisted in the soft curls as she pressed closer into his embrace.

At her response Wulff lifted her against him until her feet left the floor. Their bodies melded as each contour found its complement.

"You still love me," he murmured against her lips. "Admit it."

"Yes," she whispered. "I still love you."

Wedging her hands between them she pushed against his chest and tore her mouth away from his. He slowly released her.

"I love you," she repeated. "But trust is as important as love. And I don't trust you anymore."

She saw the pain in his eyes as her words found and pierced their mark. He quickly lowered his gaze to stare at the floor.

"Not at all?" he asked hoarsely.

"Not much," she replied. Now was the time to be completely honest, even if it hurt.

Wulff sighed deeply and looked back up at her. "Can you trust me enough to take a walk with me? There's something I have to show you."

She thought of Evans...of Michael...of weather reports and revolvers. "I don't know."

Exasperated, Wulff reached out and grasped her shoulders. His hands were so big, so powerful. She shuddered.

"Come on, Brittany." He shook her gently. "You don't really think I'd hurt you, do you? I'm the man who held you and made love to you. You felt safe in my arms, in my bed, didn't you?"

She nodded. Oh, yes. She had felt safe and loved and cherished and...

"Well, in spite of what you heard, I haven't changed. I'm still the same man and I still love you."

He took her silence as an acceptance of his declaration. "Get dressed, love, and meet me on the beach."

He turned and left the cabin, quietly closing the door behind him.

As she pulled on a pair of jeans and a red sweatshirt Brittany wondered what he could show her that would make any difference.

She felt a tiny, persistent flame of hope rekindling in her heart. She must be naive, blinded by love to hope that he could tell her or show her something that would make sense of this mess.

Quickly she ran a brush through her hair and left the cabin to join him on the beach.

The sun spread its delicate yellow fingers across the sky. The ocean was the calmest that it had been since she had arrived, and the soft morning light reflected on its glassine surface.

She stood beside Wulff and looked out across the water, trying to absorb some of its peace and serenity.

Turning toward him she found him watching her with something like guilt dulling his eyes. "I'm ready," she said, ignoring how the rays of the sun lit the auburn highlights of his mussed hair.

"Are you?" he asked quietly. "I wonder...."

He started walking down the beach in the opposite direction from the lighthouse. "Come on, love. We've got a bit of a hike ahead of us."

They walked in silence for nearly half an hour until they reached a rocky point that stretched from the land, across the beach and out into the water. The walls of jagged limestone resembled those cliffs that surrounded Wolf Cove.

Saying nothing, Aren took her hand, and they began to scale the rocks, much the same way as they had climbed into the cove the day that he had shown her the caves. Only this time, he helped her from rock to rock with only the barest minimum of conversation and physical contact.

She watched him carefully as they scrambled up the cliff. His eyes avoided hers, and his tanned brow was drawn into tight, tense lines.

As they neared the top of the cliff, the boulders became rocks and the rocks became small stones. On the top of the hill she could see tufts of grass growing on a narrow plateau.

Wulff reached the ledge and pulled her up after him. "Well, there it is," he said, pointing below him.

On the other side of the rocky bluff, Brittany could see a small, peaceful cove that at first glance, looked exactly like Wolf Cove. On second glance, she noticed that this inlet contained none of the jagged rocks that gave Wolf Cove its infamous name.

"It's the ears, the wolf's ears," she exclaimed.

"What?"

"This cove, I noticed it one day when I was looking down from the light. The island is shaped like a wolf's head, like the sign over the gate and your tattoo. Wolf Cove is the wolf's mouth and this cove is between his ears."

Aren looked as surprised as she was pleased with her discovery. "You're very observant. Most people don't notice that unless it's pointed out to them. But that's the problem with you, Nurse Brittany. You see and hear things that you aren't supposed to."

She ignored his statement and pursued her train of thought. "So, was the island named after Captain Wulff or because of its shape?"

"Its shape. It was Wolf Island long before my great-grandfather wrecked in the cove."

"But your name?"

"Coincidence," he replied curtly as though his mind were somewhere other than on her questions. Then he added, "Or providence, depending on how you look at it. Captain Jonathan thought it was a sign from heaven, so he settled here.

"This is Moonstone Cove," he said, bringing her back to the subject at hand. "It's named after the smooth, round stones that are all over the beach down there."

"It's beautiful. But why did you bring me up here?"

Wulff lowered himself to the ground and pointed to a patch of grass beside him. "Have a seat, love. This will take a while."

Brittany collapsed onto the tiny bit of turf. Aren said nothing at first, but stared at the infinite expanse of ocean that stretched before them.

"Well?" she prompted.

"Yes, well." Wulff shifted his position so that he could face her. His huge hands clasped hers and held them tightly.

"I'm going to ask you something," he said slowly. "And I want you to think about it before you answer because it's very important. Okay?"

"Okay."

"Your brother was special to you. He was the only family you had, and you loved him very much."

"That's true, but that's not a question."

"I know." He took a deep breath and traced the lines in her palm with his fingertip. "I'm getting to that." There was a moment's hesitation before he continued.

"Brittany, consider how much you loved your brother and how you feel about me. Which is the most important to you: remembering Michael as a perfect, idealistic, loving person, or having a future with me?"

She pulled her hands away from his, her topaz eyes filled with confusion. "Now what kind of a question is that?"

"A difficult one, so think about it before you answer. No matter which you choose, you're going to be giving up something that really matters to you."

"You're asking me to choose between you and my brother when I don't even know what you're talking about."

"I know you don't and I'm sorry. I don't mean to confuse you. I'm just trying to find out what you want to hear."

A long breath escaped her lips. "I'll tell you exactly what I want to hear: the truth. I can take anything you have to say, but I can't stand this uncertainty any longer."

Wulff picked up a stone from the ground beside him and pitched it into the cove. They listened as it clattered from one boulder to another until it landed noiselessly on the sandy beach below.

"So, you want the truth, the whole truth and nothing but the truth? Okay, here goes."

He closed his eyes for a moment and then looked back at her. She sat quietly waiting. The sea breeze swept her golden hair back over her shoulders.

Wulff sighed. She looked so soft, so young and vulnerable.

"Remember when I said in the telegram that Michael had been under the influence at the time of the accident?"

"Yes?"

"Well, he was under the influence, but not of alcohol. Michael was using large amounts of cocaine."

Brittany shook her head, immediately rejecting his words. "No, you must be mistaken. Michael never took drugs. He drank too much from time to time, but he never did drugs."

"I'm pretty sure that he didn't until he came down here this last time," Wulff replied. "But he got involved with a group of rather sleazy fellows in Nassau and, well, his life went downhill after that."

"What do you mean?" Something in his eyes made her reluctant to ask, but she wanted to know everything.

"Cocaine is a very expensive habit to maintain, Brittany. And Michael was an addict. He did things to support his habit that he never would have done otherwise."

Her eyes narrowed, and she was afraid of what she would hear next. "Go on," she prompted.

Wulff reached again for her hand. He held it firmly this time, not allowing her to withdraw it. "Brittany, Michael was a drug runner. In fact, he was smuggling a load of cocaine from Nassau to Miami the night that he died."

No, it couldn't be true. Not her brother. Not Michael. She opened her mouth to accuse Wulff of lying to her. But his eyes were looking straight into hers with a sincerity that she knew was genuine.

"Are you sure about this?" she asked, her voice hardly more than a whisper.

He stroked her cheek with his knuckles. His eyes were soft and full of compassion. "Brittany, I love you. I'd never tell you something like that unless I was absolutely certain."

Brittany pulled her eyes away from his and stared into the emptiness of the horizon. She felt as though the breath had been knocked out of her. In spite of the warm rays of the morning sun on her face, she felt cold and empty.

And yet, she couldn't say that she was shocked. As much as she had tried to deny it, she had known that something was wrong those last few months before Michael's death. His letters had changed somehow. She had felt that he was withdrawing, hiding something from her.

She wanted to believe that Wulff was mistaken, but her heart told her that what he was saying was true.

Why hadn't she seen it? She was Michael's sister. She should have known.

"How did you find out?" she asked.

"I'd suspected it for a long time. But I didn't know for sure until after his death. Evans told me."

"Evans?" The knot in her stomach tightened at the very thought of the man. "What did he have to do with Michael? Is he one of the drug dealers?"

"No. Evans is a jerk and I wouldn't trust him any farther than I could throw him. But he isn't what you think. He's a drug enforcement agent."

"Evans is a cop?"

"Sort of. He and his men have been trying to crack this gang of smugglers for a long time now, and they're getting impatient. The group that Michael was involved with is one of the main channels for the flow of drugs from the Bahamas to the United States."

Wulff absentmindedly ran his fingers up the seam of her jeans to her knee. "Evans was after Michael the night he died. Michael ducked into Wolf Cove to hide from Evans and his men, who were closing in on him."

Wulff's hand closed over her knee. "There was a storm that night and visibility was bad. He may have thought that he was entering this cove instead. On a dark night the two coves look a lot alike. He was high, and he knew that Evans was right behind him. He wrecked . . . on the rocks."

"But the lighthouse," she argued. "He must have seen the light—"

"If the light was on," he muttered, his jaw tight.

"But you said that Bob was keeping the—"

Brittany stopped, shocked by the look of stark anger on Wulff's face. His eyes were like blue ice, sending a chill down her spine. His hand tightened on her knee.

"Wulff? What is it?" She was nearly afraid to ask. Then suddenly, she had her answer. Everything came together in her mind. The coroner's report, "Massive brain contusion." Bob's guilt-ridden face when he had apologized for Michael's death. The way he had avoided her eyes after he had found out who she was.

The man in her dream had a face after all. "It was Bob," she whispered. "Bob killed Michael, didn't he?"

Wulff looked away. He couldn't bear to see the pain in her eyes, like a wounded animal. "Evans thinks so," he murmured. "I . . . I don't know. I've known Bob all his life. He's worked for me for three years. I hate to think that he's capable of cold-blooded murder. But it's possible."

"But why? Why would Bob want to hurt Michael?" she asked, her hands seeking the strength of his solid chest.

"Because of the drugs he was carrying. They were never recovered. And because Bob was jealous of Michael. Evans has an informant who's inside this circle of smugglers. The informant told Evans that Bob was the one who introduced Michael to the group. Apparently Bob's been in it for several years now. Michael was ambitious and eager to move up in the group, and Bob was jealous of him. Evans's informant said that they had had a big fight the day before, when Bob found out that they were giving his run to Michael."

"Would that be reason enough for him to kill my brother?" she asked.

"I'd say that their dislike for each other plus a load of cocaine worth a fortune might be enough."

Brittany closed her eyes and recalled the horror of her nightmare. "I dreamed about Michael's death last night. I was so confused...I think my mind was trying to figure it all out. I dreamed that someone killed him after he fought his way to shore, like my great-grandfather. I saw the man do it, but I didn't know it was Bob."

She closed her eyes and recalled the details of her nightmare. "He stood there for a long time, looking down at Michael, as though he were trying to decide what to do."

Wulff pitched another stone onto the beach below, where rows of lacy foam lined up three deep, waiting to wash onto the sand and dissolve.

"I can't imagine that murdering anyone would be easy for Bob," he said. "I've been watching him since Michael's death, and I can see that it's eating away at him."

Bitter hatred welled up inside Brittany. "Good," she snapped. "I hope it haunts him until the day he dies."

Wulff stood and stretched his legs. "Well, if Evans has his way, that might be sooner than you think."

"What do you mean?" she asked, as she, too, stood and brushed the dust and bits of dried grass from her jeans.

"I'm talking about what you heard up there in the lighthouse yesterday. According to Evans's informant, Bob's going to be running a load through tomorrow night. Evans wants me to help catch him."

"Catch him? Why does he need you to do that?"

Hand in hand they began to walk along the top of the narrow, rocky cliff.

"Because they've tried before and failed. The dealers in Nassau furnish their runners with cigarettes—"

"Cigarettes?"

"That's what they call those sleek, high-powered speedboats that can run circles around anything the agents have. Evans needs to catch them while they're actually transporting the drugs, but every time he tries, he loses them."

"Is that why you were talking about the false light?"

He nodded. "That's how the wreckers used to work here on the island. Sailors and navigators knew about Moonstone Cove, here. It's a safe, deep harbor in case of a storm, and there are even some nice little grottoes down there to hide in if somebody's after you."

He pointed out the dark arches in the sides of the cliff below them.

"The problem is that the entrance to Moonstone Cove looks a lot like the entrance to Wolf Cove. In a fog or a storm you can hardly tell them apart."

Her eyes surveyed the peaceful, deep waters of the cove below them. "I can see the resemblance."

"Well, that similarity helped wreckers throughout the years. All they had to do was wait for a storm or a foggy night and hope that a ship would mistakenly seek refuge in Wolf Cove. Sometimes the dirty buggers would light a lamp down by the water's edge in Wolf Cove and wait for the ship's captain to see it and think that another ship had taken refuge in the cove. They'd come in expecting a safe, deep harbor and wreck."

Brittany shuddered as she remembered her dream and her great-grandfather's ship moaning as it floundered on the rocks.

"Is that what you're going to do to Bob?" she asked with mixed emotions.

"We're going to lure him into the cove, but we'll have to use a different method because of the light. Evans is going to let him know that they're right behind him to get him rattled. Then one of Evans's men will light a false lamp on the hill just north of Wolf Cove. When I see that light, I'm supposed to kill the beacon. Supposedly, Bob will see the false lamp, assume that he's passed Wolf Cove and duck into it, thinking that he's hiding from them in Moonstone Cove. He's hidden before here in the grottoes. Evans is counting on him trying it again under pressure."

Brittany stopped walking and kicked at a tuft of grass. She desperately wanted Bob to be punished if he had killed Michael. But the horror of her dream was still fresh, and the thought of anyone else dying on those rocks, even Bob, was repulsive to her. There had been too many violent deaths in Wolf Cove already.

"So, which is Evans trying to do: catch Bob or kill him?"

Wulff's jaw tensed, and he stuffed his hands deep into his pockets. "He says he wants to catch him with the dope, but to be honest, I don't think it would bother him at all if Bob dies there on the rocks."

Brittany reached over and trailed her finger along the rough stubble on his chin. She turned his face toward hers and searched his eyes. "And how about you, Aren? Would it bother you if Bob dies in Wolf Cove?"

"Yes, Brittany, it would bother me," he said slowly. "After all, I'm a lighthouse keeper. My life has been dedicated to saving people from that cove.

"But," he continued in a deeper, more ominous tone, "when I think about Bob murdering Michael with his bare hands, I'm willing to do it. I trusted him to watch the light. If he betrayed that trust and killed my friend, I'm not sure that I care very much what happens to him."

He pulled his hands from his pockets and placed them on her shoulders. "How about you, love? Michael was your brother. How do you feel about it?"

One step forward brought her into the circle of his arms. She pressed her face against the front of his shirt. "I want Bob to be punished. A large part of me even wants to see him dead. But the cove...the rocks. I don't know. I have mixed feelings about it."

She sighed as she wound her arms around his waist. "I'm so glad that you're still the man that I thought you were. After hearing you and Evans yesterday, I thought—"

"I know what you thought, love," he said, chuckling softly. "I remember that you made it quite clear at the time."

The harsh words that she had spoken the day before came back, overwhelming her with shame. She had said such terrible things to him when he had only been trying to avoid hurting her.

"Aren, I'm so sorry." Brittany lifted her hands and gently stroked his forehead where a feathering of tiny curls blew in the breeze. "Please, forgive me," she whispered, her fingers continuing their exploration across the fullness of his lower lip.

How could he resist this woman whose touch excited every fiber of his being? This goddess who held the golden sunlight in her eyes and hair?

His arms tightened around her waist, pulling her even closer to him. His lips grazed the top of her sunwarmed hair, then traveled down her temple and lower, where he tenderly nuzzled her ear.

"I don't blame you, sweetheart. I really don't," he whispered, his moist breath caressing her neck. "I would have thought the same thing. Anyone would have. Are we okay now?"

In answer she lifted her face to his and pulled his head down. At the touch of his lips on hers, a tremendous feeling of relief surged through her.

Wulff wasn't a monster after all. He was what she thought he was, a good man who loved her and—

The thoughts flew out of her mind as blithely as the seabirds that soared above them. Brittany released every thought, every feeling except that of his warm lips on hers, the scent and taste of him, the sound of his soft moan as she parted her lips and invited him inside.

He held her tighter, more desperately than he ever had before. They had nearly lost each other, and they both felt the need to reestablish the bonds that had been so severely strained.

The flames of passion flared quickly, fueled by their joy at being reconciled.

"Aren, I want you," she murmured against his neck, as she slipped her hands beneath his shirt and massaged the corded muscles of his back.

He laughed lightly and followed suit, gliding his big, warm hands under the soft fleece of her sweatshirt.

"Be more specific, love," he whispered wickedly. "You already have me, heart and soul. What more could you want? Let's see," he mused, running his fingers over the lace cups of her bra. "Maybe you want this." His thumbs found the sensitive peaks of her nipples and massaged them into hardened points.

"Or maybe some of this." Slowly his hands moved down to cup her hips and press her pelvis tightly against

his. Waves of desire flooded over her as she felt the
hardness of his arousal through their clothes.

"You're always teasing me," Brittany said. "You
know exactly what I want." She pulled back slightly
and smiled at him. "Let's go back to my cabin."

Chapter Eleven

Like two eager children hurrying to a birthday party, Brittany and Aren rushed back to the tiny cottage on the beach. The return trip took only twenty minutes instead of thirty and was punctuated with several of his earthy suggestions and her answering laughter and blushes.

When they reached the cabin, they burst through the door and fell, laughing, on the daybed.

"Well, I'll be damned. You're ticklish, Nurse Brittany," Wulff exclaimed, running his fingers along her ribs.

"I—am—not," she choked, squirming beneath his weight.

He lifted her sweatshirt and revealed her bare midriff. "Oh, okay. So you won't mind if I do this." Growling deep in his throat he began to not so gently nibble the flesh on her ribs.

"No," she screamed. "Stop it, don't!"

She grabbed his shoulders and pushed with all her might. Caught off guard, Wulff rolled sideways and tumbled off the bed. As he fell, he pulled her with him, and they landed in a giggling, twisted heap on the floor.

"I swear, lady, you're a handful for such a little thing," Wulff exclaimed, looking up at her. She lay over him, her long hair streaming down into his face. His hand ran up the front of her sweatshirt and paused to knead her breast. "A very nice handful, I might add."

Brittany raised her face from his and looked around. "We're, ah; on the floor."

"Yeah, I noticed," he replied dryly.

"The floor's still damp."

"I noticed that, too."

She lifted herself off him and rose to her feet. "Wanna try the bed again?"

He stood beside her and looked around the room. "Well, we don't have much choice, unless you want to do it on the table. Ever do it on a table before?"

"You've got to be kidding."

"No, really, it's kinda fun. There's this pub over in Nassau and one night after they closed—"

She clamped a hand over his mouth. "I don't want to hear any of your decadent stories." She laughed.

Wulff studied the rickety legs of the table thoughtfully. "Well, maybe I'll let you know about it some other time—with some other table."

His smile faded as he slowly walked over to the table. Her eyes followed his, and she saw it lying there next to her opened suitcase—a large, manila envelope.

"Is this it?" he asked solemnly.

"Is it what?" she replied, trying to think of something to draw his attention from that damned packet. Oh, God, why hadn't she put it away after she had looked at it yesterday?

Wulff lifted the envelope from the table and read the London address. "Is this the incriminating evidence against my family that you were telling me about yesterday?"

"Aren, give it to me, please." She held out her hand.

Guardedly his eyes searched hers. "I was going to ask you about it anyway. Now's as good a time as any." He reached inside the envelope and pulled out a handful of photocopies.

"Wulff, don't!" she cried, snatching at the papers. "Damn it, those are mine, and you have no right to read them if I ask you not to."

He held the documents out of her reach for a moment, then reconsidered. "All right," he said, handing the papers to her. "They're yours, and I won't read them if you don't want me to. But if they contain information about my family, I think I have a right to know what they say."

Brittany clutched the copies to her chest and slowly walked away from him. She sat on the end of the bed, silent as she tried to decide what to do.

Still holding the envelope, Wulff sat on the opposite end of the bed. "Well?" he coaxed.

"Well, what?"

"You know what. Do those papers mention my family? Captain Jonathan to be exact?"

She swallowed a lump in her throat. "Yes."

His eyes narrowed. "You made some rather serious accusations against him yesterday and said that you had some proof. Are those documents your proof?"

She nodded, her eyes not meeting his.

"And you're not going to let me see them?"

Clutching the papers tighter to her chest she shook her head.

"Do you really think that's fair, Brittany?" he asked.

"It's not a question of what's fair."

"Then why won't you let me see them?"

"For the same reason that you didn't want to tell me about Michael," she said with a quiver in her voice.

Wulff's face softened as he leaned over and stroked her cheek. "Are you trying to protect me, sweetheart, trying to spare my feelings?"

She lifted her golden eyes to his; they glittered with tears. "Yes," she whispered.

He sighed and leaned back against the pillows, toying with the envelope in his hands. "When I tried to protect you from the truth, we ran into all kinds of problems. I'm glad now that I told you about Michael. You handled it better than I thought you would."

"Yes, but that's because I knew that something was wrong all along. I wasn't expecting to hear that he was a drug runner, but I was sort of prepared for it. That's why I wasn't devastated."

"And you think that this information of yours will devastate me, because I'm not prepared for it?" he asked.

"It might. Oh, Aren, you're so proud of your heritage and you have good reason to be. Your parents were heroes who gave their lives to save others. And you've risked your own life to pull people out of those waters. You're a proud man, and I don't want to take that away from you."

Wulff sat quietly, thinking about what she had said. He turned the envelope over, and an antique pocket watch fell into his hand. Absently he ran his fingertip along the deep engravings that were carved on its gold case.

"I understand what you're saying, Brittany. And I appreciate your concern for my feelings. But if my pride is based on lies, I need to know that. Besides, after what you said yesterday, I have a pretty good idea what's in those papers, anyway."

She hung her head. "I'm so sorry that I said anything to you. I'll never forgive myself for that."

His fingers found the catch on the side of the watch, and the timepiece sprang open at his touch. The silence of the room was instantly broken by the tinkling notes of a simple but charming melody from its miniature music box.

Inside the engraved cover was the picture of a beautiful woman with long blond curls spilling over her white shoulders and down onto the lace of her old-fashioned gown.

"She's very pretty," Wulff said, studying the picture. "Who is she?"

"That's my great-grandmother, Elizabeth Davis," Brittany replied. "The museum sent the watch to me when they mailed the documents. The wrecker had it in his possession when he was arrested, and the curator thought that it would be better if I had it than for it to be lying around on a shelf in their archives."

"That was very thoughtful of him." Wulff squinted at the picture, his brow furrowed in thought. "She looks familiar somehow."

He glanced up at Brittany and then back at the picture. "I guess she looks a bit like you. Not as pretty, though."

With a sudden movement he closed the cover and the music stopped. He placed the watch on the bed between them and held out his hand. "Come on, love, you're not the one hurting me. You've warned me, and it's my decision. I want to read those papers."

Brittany stared at his open palm. With a sigh of resignation she laid the papers in his hand, rose from the daybed and walked away from him toward the window.

She didn't want to see his face when he read that the hero of Wolf Island, the great-grandfather that he idolized, had cooperated with the wreckers. That Jonathan Wulff had turned out his lamp, enabling the moon cursers to lure Stephen Davis to the rocks of the cove. His ship, the *Lady Elizabeth*, had been torn apart on the rocks; Captain Davis and his entire crew had perished in the sea, or were murdered by the wreckers after they fought their way to the shore.

The records showed that Captain Wulff had delivered the moon cursers to the authorities and had been granted amnesty for his part in the crime in exchange for his testimony against the gang.

The wreckers were hung, and the ship's cargo was never recovered.

The authorities had carefully monitored Captain Wulff's activities until the day he died, one year to the day after the wreck of the *Lady Elizabeth*. But there were no other incidents in Wolf Cove.

Brittany gazed out the window at the shining pinnacle of white that was Wolf Light. That was where it all had happened, so long ago.

For the first time, the past seemed insignificant to her. Why should the present be clouded by events that occurred more than a century before? Why should Wulff suffer for something that his ancestor did, a man he had never even known?

He shouldn't. It doesn't matter, she thought. None of it: the treasure, the wreckers, even Michael's dream. None of it seemed important anymore.

The only things that mattered to Brittany were Aren, Jesse, Debra and her new baby. They were the present and the future.

The heavy silence that hung in the room was occasionally interrupted by the sound of Wulff turning the pages. Brittany listened, anxiously wondering which passage he was reading and how it was affecting him.

Finally she turned around and saw him sitting quietly, leaning forward with his head down and his elbows resting on his knees. The papers lay in a pile on the bed beside him.

"Aren?" she said softly as she crossed the room and knelt next to the bed.

He glanced over at the watch on the rumpled sheets beside him. Picking it up, he turned it over in his hand and released the clasp. Once again the melody filled the room. Its cheerful tones mocked them.

"He was her husband," Wulff murmured as he looked at the picture.

"What?" she asked, leaning her head closer to him.

"Captain Jonathan turned out the lamp and killed her husband."

"Aren," she whispered, gently taking the watch from his hand. "It's all right. It's in the past and it doesn't matter anymore."

"She looked like you, Brittany. He was your great-grandfather."

Wulff abruptly stood and walked to the door.

"But, Aren," she called out, staring after him. "Where are you going? Are you okay?"

"Yes, I'm okay. I just want to be alone for a while. I'm sorry, love," he said as his hand closed over the knob.

A moment later, he was gone.

Brittany paced the floor of the tiny cabin, walked on the beach and checked Debra and the baby. She did everything she could think of, except what she wanted to do—go up to the lighthouse.

More than anything, she wanted to be with Aren, to see how he was coping and help in any way she could. But he'd told her that he needed time alone to sort out his thoughts and feelings, so she spent the afternoon condemning herself and worrying about him.

About sundown, she lost the battle. Finding the front tire of Debra's bicycle flat, she decided to walk the scenic route to the light.

After all, the worst thing Wulff could do to her was ask her to leave. Anything, she decided, would be better than this terrible waiting and wondering.

The natural beauty of the sea was lost on Brittany as she left the cabin behind her and walked along the beach toward Wolf Rock. Her troubled thoughts allowed no room for her to appreciate the rosy glow of the setting sun or the way it painted the shimmering sands at her feet with delicate shades of mauve.

Her only thoughts were of what she would say to Wulff when she saw him again. She had to find a way to repair the damage she had done.

The sun sank below the horizon as she scrambled down the rocky cliff into the cove. Glancing up, she didn't see anyone in the lighthouse.

As she walked along the path toward the house, she heard someone call her name. Turning around, she saw Wulff come out of the boat house with a hammer in one hand and a kerosene lantern in the other.

Expecting to find him distraught, she was pleased and curious to see what he was doing. She hurried down the path and ran along the beach to meet him.

"You're just in time," he exclaimed. His face was flushed, and his eyes sparkled with excitement. "I was going to come and get you. You've got to see this."

"See what?" she asked, following at his heels.

"It may not be anything at all, but I have a feeling—"

"What? What are you talking about?"

"Come on, in here."

Wulff led her into the smallest cave, the one near the cove entrance. In the dim light she saw that he had assembled a collection of tools: a shovel, a pick, an ax, several flashlights and another kerosene lamp.

Fumbling in his pocket, he produced a small metal matchbox, struck a match and lit the two lanterns. The light flickered, casting eery, dancing shadows on the cave's rugged walls. From the back wall a small steel pipe protruded about five feet.

"What are you doing in here?" Brittany asked, running her hand along the pipe.

"It was that picture, the one of your great-grandmother," he said breathlessly. "I knew she looked familiar."

Setting the lanterns on the dark floor, he grabbed the hammer and began pounding on the end of the pipe.

"Can you hang on to this, about there?" he said, pointing to the length of pipe next to the wall. "Just steady it a bit while I—that's it."

"Do you mind telling me what we're doing?" she asked as the vibrations from his blows traveled up the pipe into her hands and arms.

"Sure, the picture of your great-grandmother, it's the same as the figurehead."

"What figurehead?"

"The one I found in this cave about five years ago after the hurricane."

"What hurricane?" she shouted above the din that echoed in the darkness around them. Her patience was wearing thin.

"What?" he shouted.

"What—" He stopped hammering and she lowered her voice. "What are you talking about? Explain, now."

Wulff sighed and lowered his hammer. "About five years ago Hurricane Gwendolynn swept through here. The waves were tremendous. They even came up into this cave. Part of this back wall was torn down."

He waved his arm toward the wall and the pipe. "I found a figurehead, you know, from the front of a ship, buried in the debris. It was your great-grandmother Davis. I mean, it looked just like her, like the picture in the watch. That's where I'd seen her before. The figurehead. See?"

"I think so, but why are we doing this?" she asked.

"Because, in those papers of yours, the wrecker said that they hid the cargo from the *Lady Elizabeth* in one of these caves. I was thinking that if I found the figurehead in here, it might have been this cave."

"That makes sense, but why the pipe?"

Wulff took a deep breath and ran his fingers through his dark mane. "I thought that maybe this cave has a second room, like the big one does. Maybe this isn't the back of this cave at all, but a wall with a room on the other side. It's probably a crazy idea, but it's worth a try."

Brittany watched his eyes glitter in the lamplight. His breathing was ragged and a sheen of sweat glistened on his muscular arms. The thin fabric of his shirt clung to the moisture on his chest and back.

"I thought you didn't care about treasure anymore," she said, "that it was a dream you'd given up."

His gaze swept over her, conveying a primitive message that caused her to shiver. "I'd given up on you, too, but look at what a treasure I found."

She glanced away, feeling the old blush again in her cheeks. "So," she said, changing the subject, "you're driving this pipe into the wall to see if it's solid?"

"That's right. Hang on and let's see if we break through."

Once again he commenced hammering on the end of the pipe. She held it steady, absorbing the shock of his blows until her hands and arms tingled from the reverberations. Inch by inch the pipe slid through her hands and disappeared into the cave wall.

"I've already tried in four or five places," he shouted, "but I kept running into rock. This place seems softer."

"How far in has the pipe gone?"

"About two and a half or three feet. That's about how thick the back wall is in the other—"

Wulff let out a long, low whistle as with one final blow the pipe shot through their hands and disap-

peared into the wall. Only a few inches of the length
remained in view.

"Hot damn, Nurse Brittany, we did it!" he exclaimed. "There's a space of some kind in there."

Brittany rubbed her hands where the pipe had slid
through them. "You were really pounding on that
sucker."

"I had to. That wall's made of rock and compacted
dirt. Are you all right?"

"Sure," she said, wiping her hands on her jeans. "I
wasn't expecting it, that's all. If the wall is that hard,
how are we going to get through it?"

Wulff picked up a shovel. "*We* aren't going to.
You've already done your part. All I have to do is clear
a hole large enough to crawl through."

Brittany watched as he attacked the solid wall with
a shovel and pick. It was hard work, with progress
made in inches, yet Wulff dug at a feverish pace.

Caught up in his excitement, she felt her pulse race
with anticipation. It was difficult to remember that
only that afternoon she had decided the hope of finding treasure was an empty dream. It did matter after
all, this dream of Michael's . . . and Wulff's.

Her eyes scanned the wall. There was something behind it. She could feel it. "The opening that you're
trying to dig—is it about that big?" she asked, pointing to a large rock embedded in the base of the wall.

Wulff stopped and leaned, panting, on his shovel.
"Yes, as a matter of fact, that's about the size I had in
mind. Do you think we could move it?"

"We could try. It can't be much more difficult than
what you're trying to do now."

Wulff surveyed the tiny hole that his labor had produced. "That's for damn sure," he replied, throwing the shovel to the ground.

They knelt together in front of the stone and Wulff ran his fingers along its edges. "You know, it looks to me like we could pry this out with a crowbar. Did I bring one of those along with me?"

Brittany looked among the pile of tools that he had assembled. "Right here," she said, handing him the iron bar. "You use this and I'll use the shovel."

Wulff positioned the pointed end of the crowbar at the edge of the stone and hammered on the other end, driving the point between the dirt and the rock. Then he tossed the hammer aside and threw his weight against the bar again and again, trying to rock the stone loose.

"That bloody bugger is really stuck fast in there," he said, grunting with effort.

Suddenly the rock shifted, and a small crevice appeared between the stone and the dirt that surrounded it. Brittany thrust the shovel into the opening and joined him in prying the stone from its place in the wall.

Once the rock was loose, some pushing and straining rolled it free.

"Look at that, love," Wulff exclaimed when he caught his breath. "Just look at that."

He pointed to a black, gaping hole in the wall where the rock had been. Brittany sank to the ground, her legs shaking from exertion.

"There's a draft coming out of there," she said, leaning down to stare into the pitch-blackness inside.

"That's good. That means there's ventilation of some kind and we'll be able to breathe. Come on, let's see what's in there."

He noted the uneasy look on her face as she peered into the darkness. "I'll go first. If anything gets me, it's been nice knowing you, kid."

"That's not funny."

"Sorry, it's the best I could do on short notice. Hand me that torch and step aside."

She placed the flashlight in his hand and moved out of his way. Wulff stopped to toss the shovel through the hole.

"Insurance," he muttered, "in case the wall comes down while we're in there."

"Nice thought," she replied.

Wulff knelt before the opening and squeezed his shoulders through. In a second he had disappeared into the darkness.

"What do you see?" she asked, leaning down to the hole.

"Nothing."

"Nothing?"

"Yeah, I've got my eyes closed. No, wait a minute—"

"Yes? What is it?"

"They were open. It's just bloody dark in here."

She released an exasperated sigh. "Oh, for heaven's sake, Wulff. What's in there?"

"I tell you, I don't know. Come on in and bring the lantern with you. The batteries in this torch are dead."

Brittany grabbed another flashlight and the kerosene lamp and crawled through the hole.

Large hands reached down for her and pulled her to her feet. The lantern's feeble glow illuminated a room that was not even half as large as the second room of the big cave.

Wulff took the flashlight from her and shone its piercing beam into the gloomy recesses of the chamber. "I can't believe this has been here all these years and we never knew it."

Brittany grabbed the lantern from his hand. "Look, over there." She pointed the beam toward the far corner. The light bounced back at them from a large wooden object.

"Here," he said, handing her the flashlight. "Give me the lamp."

He took the lantern from her and turned up the wick, increasing its flame. They both gasped when they saw a dozen or more large crates lined up against the far wall of the room.

"What . . . what are they?" she asked breathlessly.

"I don't know for sure, but I have a pretty good idea," he said as he quickly crossed the room and knelt beside one of the containers.

Brittany shone her light on the side of the case, illuminating its bold, black lettering: ENFIELD/24.

"What the heck's an Enfield 24?" she asked.

Wulff said nothing, but ran his hand over the rough surface of the wooden crate.

"Aren't we going to open it and see what's inside?" she asked impatiently.

"I know what's inside," he muttered. "You can get through that hole easier than I can. Would you go back out there and get me the crowbar and the hatchet? Be careful, it's sharp."

"Sure." Brittany hesitated, then disappeared. She quickly returned carrying the tools.

With the crowbar Wulff pried away the lid of the crate. Inside they found a large metal case.

"What is it?" she asked again.

"It's a tin-lined wooden crate. And the lid's still soldered closed. That's good. They should still be in good condition."

"Who's still in good condition?" she asked as he hacked away at the top of the tin case with the hatchet.

"These," he said finally, peeling back the tin as though he were opening the top of a giant sardine can. "Enfield rifled muskets."

Carefully reaching into the case, he removed a long object, swathed in linen strips. Unwinding the cloth wrappings, he revealed a gleaming musket.

"Here you go, love," he said, holding it out to her. "It's a beauty and perfectly preserved."

Brittany cringed and stepped back. "I don't like guns, never have."

"Well, fortunately for you, some people do. In fact, in Miami you could probably get close to a thousand dollars for this one rifle. And there are twenty-three more like it in this crate alone."

She did a bit of quick arithmetic in her head as she counted more than a dozen crates along the wall. "My God," she whispered.

"That's right. Congratulations, Nurse Brittany. You're a wealthy lady."

Her knees were suddenly too weak to hold her; she sat down on the nearest crate.

"*I'm* wealthy?" she said. "How about you? You found these, too. Besides, they're on your property."

Wulff kicked at the nearest loose board. As the sound reverberated off the cave's walls she saw some of the pain of that afternoon stealing back into his face.

"These guns were your great-grandfather's cargo, the cargo that Captain Jonathan stole from him. You don't really think that I'd want any of it, do you?"

"But I would never have found it if it weren't for you, Aren. Besides, I thought you and I were into sharing these days."

"Well, we can argue about that later," he said, lifting the corner of each crate.

"What do we have here?" he asked, as he bent down and lifted a small metal box from between two crates. He opened its creaky, hinged lid.

Brittany brought her flashlight and shone it down into the box. "It looks like a book, an old leather book of some kind."

Wulff lifted the tome from its resting place and laid the box on one of the crates. He carefully thumbed through the yellowed pages. "It looks like a journal."

Suddenly, as though it had burned his fingers, he threw it against the wall. The book landed with a soft thud on the dirt floor. "It is a journal," he muttered through gritted teeth. "It's his journal."

"Whose?" she asked. "Captain Jonathan's?"

Wulff turned on his heel and strode back to the opening in the wall.

"Aren?" she called after him. "Wait a minute. You can't throw it away like that."

"I don't want the damned thing, okay? I don't even want to look at it."

Brittany watched as he disappeared through the hole, leaving her alone in the room. She picked the book out of the dust and held it in her hand, feeling its soft leather binding.

It almost felt alive, vibrant. It seemed to radiate the same vitality that she felt when she touched Wulff.

She couldn't leave it there in the cave. Quickly she placed the book inside her shirt and followed Wulff.

Chapter Twelve

What's the matter? Aren't you hungry?" Brittany asked as Wulff shoved his half-eaten plate of fried conch away and leaned his elbows on the table.

He rubbed his face wearily. "I guess I'm too tired to eat."

She leaned across the table and took his hand. "It's no wonder you're exhausted. You haven't slept well since—"

"Since a certain person with long blond hair and big—" his eyes traveled down the front of her shirt "—eyes," he continued, "arrived on the island. Not mentioning any names, of course."

Brittany glanced away and cleared her throat. "As I was saying, you haven't gotten a full night's sleep in ages and the past twenty-four hours have been a bit trying, at best."

"That's for sure," he agreed with a sigh, and leaned back in his chair. A slow, easy smile spread across his handsome features. "But I'm glad we're friends again. That's what really counts. And I'm glad we found that cargo. It feels good to be able to return it to the Davis family, even if Captain Davis will never know it."

Brittany toyed with a crust of bread that she had set aside for Harvey. "I wouldn't be so sure that he doesn't know. I think Captain Davis will rest easier now. And Captain Jonathan, too."

Wulff's face hardened and he crossed his arms defensively across his chest. The wolf's head gleamed against his tanned biceps.

"You'll have to pardon me, but I don't give a damn whether Captain Jonathan rests in peace or not. In fact, I'd just as soon think that he's still tormented by what he did. I hope he's down there in the cove, rubbing elbows with his victims. That's where he died, you know."

Brittany felt a cold shiver trickle down her spine. "No, I didn't. How did it happen?"

"Nobody knows for sure. One night he left the light and walked down to the cove and straight into the water. He drowned before his wife could fish him out. It happened exactly one year after the wreck of the *Lady Elizabeth*. Funny, I'd never noticed that until today."

His long fingers flicked at some bread crumbs beside his plate. "Maybe Stephen Davis and 'him of de hands' lured Captain Jonathan down there and pulled him under."

Brittany searched his face to see if he was kidding, but she saw no trace of humor, only grim bitterness.

"Maybe the guilt became too heavy a burden for him to bear," she offered quietly.

"Whatever," he said, cutting off the topic of conversation. He pushed back his chair, stood and began gathering their empty plates. "I think I'll get these dishes done and check the light so I can call it a day. You're right. I'm beat."

Brittany stood and took the plates from him. "Let me do that. Go check your light and relax a bit."

He hesitated, then said, "All right, if you insist. A hot shower would feel good."

His eyes smiled warmly at her, crinkling in the corners. "And you can be sure that I really am dead tired, because I'm not even asking you to join me."

Her eyes returned his warmth. "That's okay. I'll join you later. That is, if I'm invited to spend another night."

"If you're invited? Of course you are." Wulff took the dishes from her hand and set them on the table. "Sweetheart, give me a hug," he said, holding out his arms to her. "I really need one right now."

She quickly stepped into his arms. Leaning her head back, she looked up into his eyes and saw a depth of longing that she had never seen before. The need that she saw reflected there had little to do with physical appetites. It was a deeper hunger of the soul, a desire of his heart rather than his body.

Brittany wound her arms around his waist and pulled him to her, molding her body to fit his.

She slid one hand up his chest to his neck, where her fingers toyed with the soft wisps of hair that curled over his collar. "I'm sorry you're so tired and that you're feeling bad. But I do love you, if that helps at all."

His arms tightened, crushing her to him until she could scarcely breathe. For a long time he held her, saying nothing. Then he kissed the top of her head, and in a voice so quiet that she scarcely heard him, he murmured, "It helps, love. More than you can imagine."

She lifted her face to look up at him, and his lips touched hers. His kiss was incredibly soft and gentle. It lacked the fiery passion of their previous kisses, but was rich with tenderness and affection. Brittany realized that, perhaps even more than the others they had shared, this kiss was from the man's heart.

She felt a shudder run through his body and wondered if it was from fatigue or emotion.

A moment later, she had her answer when he whispered, "I love you, too, Brittany. I loved you the moment I first saw you, and I'll love you till the day I die."

He pulled away and held her at arm's length. "And as far as you staying with me tonight, that's an open invitation. Nothing would make me happier than to think that I could go to sleep every night with you in my arms and wake up every morning to find you beside me."

"Then maybe we can work something out when this is all over," she said a bit breathlessly.

"I hope so." Running his finger along her cheek, he sighed deeply. "I do hope so."

Brittany dried her hands on the snowy white dish towel and hung it on an oak rod beside the sink. She left the kitchen and walked into the living room. She was beginning to feel her own fatigue as it weakened the muscles in her calves and caused a dull ache in her lower back.

With a weary groan she settled into the sofa. The sound of running water drifted down to her from upstairs. Wulff was still in the shower.

Her curiosity got the best of her; she couldn't wait any longer. Slipping her hand behind one of the pillows, she pulled out the leather journal. She had stashed it there when she had gone upstairs to shower before dinner.

The dark brown leather was soft and supple in her hand. She studied the outline of the wolf's head that was engraved on the cover and wondered if the captain himself had carved the leather.

The opened book released the musty scent of moldy paper. But all in all, the journal was in excellent condition, considering that it had spent the past century hidden away in a sea cave.

She turned the pages and marveled at the bold, slanting script written with a pen that occasionally dropped spots of ink in the margins. If handwriting was a statement of one's character, she would surmise that Captain Jonathan Wulff was an energetic, confident, aggressive man, much like his great-grandson.

Just as Brittany settled down to read some of the dated entries, she heard Wulff coming down the stairs. Once again, she shoved the journal into its hiding place behind the cushion. She didn't really think that he would mind her reading it, but she knew that it would hurt him to see the book again.

"Feel better?" she asked as he entered the room and sat beside her on the sofa.

"Much," he said. "Smell better, too. I wasn't fit company for man nor beast."

"Fortunately I was neither."

"You were neither what?" he asked.

"Man nor beast. So, I found you delightful company."

His eyes swept over her figure with that look that never failed to give her the shivers. "That's for sure," he agreed. Moving closer, he wrapped one arm around her and pulled her against him.

"You know," he whispered into her ear, "about halfway through that shower, I started to really miss you."

"You did, huh?" She breathed in the clean, crisp scent of his freshly bathed body and ran her hand along his smoothly shaven jaw.

"Yeah, I started thinking that if you were there with me I could see how your body feels . . . all wet and slippery. . . ." His hand moved over her hip and upward to cup her breast.

He nuzzled her neck with his lips while his hand fondled the heavy softness. "You know, love, if you get tired of me pawing you like this, all you have to do is say so, and I promise that I'll try to be good."

"Good?" she whispered as she reached down and lifted the front of her shirt. "Now why would I want you to be good?" She unsnapped the front clasp of her bra and pulled one of the cups aside.

She took his hand and placed it over her breast. "Why settle for good when your bedside manners and technique are . . . excellent?" she added breathlessly.

Wulff moaned as he stroked the delicate skin that she had bared for him. "My God, Nurse Brittany," he whispered, "you're my kind of woman: incredibly soft and luscious, and you possess that one special quality that every man looks for in a female."

"And what's that?" she murmured, running her hands through his still damp curls.

"Decadence, my dear. Pure, elemental decadence."

Brittany chuckled and leaned back into the cushions. "Come here, Mr. Wulff, and Little Red Riding Hood will show you the real reason why that big, bad fellow was stalking her through the woods that day."

She moved slightly and the other cup of her bra slipped aside. "I'll give you a hint," she added coyly. "It wasn't her cookies."

Wulff gazed at her, his mouth hanging slightly open. "Hot damn," he muttered, lowering his body over hers and taking the tip of her breast between his teeth. He nibbled gently, causing her to writhe beneath him with pleasure. Then he shifted his weight so that he could reach the zipper of her jeans.

"Ow! What the—" he exclaimed as something poked his side.

Reaching into the cushions, he pulled the journal out by its offending corner. "How did this get here?" he asked. One look at Brittany's red face gave him the answer.

"You—you said that you didn't want to read it," she stammered. "That doesn't mean that I can't."

He sat up on the edge of the sofa. "No, I guess it doesn't," he muttered as he tossed the book onto the pine chest.

"Are you angry?" she asked, fastening her bra and pulling her shirt into place.

"Yes, but I realize I have no right to be. You can read it if you want to. I just don't want to have to look at it or touch it or—"

Sitting up beside him, she placed one hand on his forearm. "Are you really that bitter toward him?"

Wulff jerked his arm away from her and stood. "Yes, damn it, I am. Can't you understand how I feel?

All my life I thought that Captain Jonathan was a hero, a man who saved people's lives. Then I find out that he's a bloody wrecker, the epitome of all that's evil to a light keeper.

"I grew up on stories about him and about finding pirate's treasure. Then I finally uncover a fortune and instead of being happy about it, it makes me sick, because it confirms what those damned papers of yours said. Can't you see that?" His eyes pleaded for her understanding.

"Yes, of course, I do, Aren," she said quietly. "I'm sorry I brought the book in. I should have left it in the cave."

The harsh lines of his face softened a bit. "That's okay. I know you didn't mean any harm. It's only natural that you'd be curious." He took a flashlight from the mahogany cupboard and walked toward the front door.

"I'm going to go push that rock back into the wall. We don't want anybody going in there and messing with that stuff before we get a chance to move it."

"Don't you need any help?"

"No, I can manage," he said, opening the door.

"Aren." She rose, walked over to him and wrapped her arms around his neck. "I'm worried about you."

He smiled down at her. His lips curled at the edges, but his eyes were filled with pain. "Don't worry. I'm okay," he said before he kissed her lightly on the forehead and disappeared into the darkness.

For over an hour Brittany sat with her head bent over Captain Jonathan's journal. The golden glow of the lamp lit the penned words that stirred a wide range of feelings in her heart: anger, shock, pity and, above all, incredible sadness.

When she finally laid the book aside, she rubbed her eyes and looked at the brass clock on the wall. Brittany knew what she had to do.

After searching the lighthouse and the yard, she finally found Wulff in the cove, sitting on the beach before a small fire that he had built in the sand.

His arms were wrapped around his knees and his dark head was bowed. The flickering blaze cast an orange glow over his skin and lit his hair with sparkling bits of amber.

He didn't notice her until she was only a few feet from him. Lifting his head, he looked up and saw her standing quietly over him, the light from the fire illuminating her face and golden hair.

"Wulff?" she said softly. "May I join you, or do you want to be alone?"

He held out his hand to her and pulled her down onto the sand beside him. "I've been alone too long already. I'm glad you came."

She held his hand between hers, lifted it and kissed his callused palm. "You may not be when you hear what I've come to say."

Wulff frowned, but he didn't withdraw his hand. "I suppose you've been reading that damned book," he said.

"As a matter of fact I have, and we have to talk about it."

He stared at her briefly, then turned away to gaze into the fire. "So, talk."

"Aren, your great-grandfather... he was a lot like you."

Wulff chuckled mirthlessly. "Well, hell, now I feel a lot better. Thanks for telling me that."

Brittany ignored his sarcasm and continued. "Really, he wasn't a monster. Captain Jonathan was a man who loved his wife and read stories to his sons and took meticulous care of the light, just like you. You should read the things he wrote about his family and the people on this island. He was devoted to them, like you are."

Wulff picked up a stick and tossed it into the fire. A column of tiny sparks rose in the smoke. "Then why did he wreck that ship and God knows how many others?"

"The *Lady Elizabeth* was the only one. And I understand now why he did it. He did the wrong thing for all the right reasons."

Wulff turned from the fire to glare at her. "What reasons? There's no excuse for wrecking a ship. None."

"That's what I thought, too, until I read the journal. Did you know that Captain Jonathan was originally from Connecticut?"

"Yes, I knew that. What does that have to do with it?"

"Everything," she replied. "Did you know that the captain's two younger brothers were killed in the Civil War, fighting for the North?"

Wulff lowered his head and toyed with a small stick at his feet. "No," he said quietly. "I didn't know that."

"Captain Jonathan was devastated when he received word that both of his brothers had been killed. Then only a week later, a man came to him, posing as an agent of the Union Army. This man told the captain that a ship would be sailing through here in a couple of weeks, carrying a large cargo of guns. He asked

Captain Wulff if he would help them capture the ship by putting out the light.

"He assured the captain that he and his men would do everything they could to rescue the crew and take them as prisoners of war. He said that they were only interested in seizing the weapons before they could be smuggled to the Confederate Army. You see, my great-grandfather Davis was a Southerner and a blockade-runner."

Brittany stopped to catch her breath. She scanned Wulff's face to see how he was receiving her words. But he continued to stare impassively at the stick in his hand.

"Captain Jonathan thought he was doing the right thing, Aren, really he did. He thought that by helping them he could hasten the end of the fighting and save lives. To him it was an act of war, not of greed."

Wulff poked at the fire with the stick, and they watched silently as the blaze flared, then died down.

"This man," he said finally, "the Union Army agent . . . he was a wrecker?"

"Yes, but Captain Jonathan didn't know it until that night when they began killing the ship's crew that made it to shore. By then it was too late."

She paused long enough to swallow the lump in her throat. "He never got over the guilt, Wulff. He turned the moon cursers in to the authorities and testified against them. He even gave away a fortune in medical supplies that was aboard the ship to the first block-ade-runner that he could find in Nassau. He hid the guns in the cave so they couldn't be used to prolong the war. But no matter what he did, the wreck of the *Lady Elizabeth* haunted him until the day he died. After reading the journal, I'd say that his death was a suicide.''

Wulff looked at the reflection of the full moon that glistened on the dark waters of the cove. "Suicide or vengeance," he muttered grimly.

High above them, Wolf Light cast its piercing beam to the ends of the dark horizon. As Wulff's eyes followed its circuit, he said, "Doesn't it seem strange to you that all of this information surfaces on the eve before I'm supposed to do the same thing?"

"What do you mean?"

"Tomorrow night, I'm going to turn the light out again for the first time in over a hundred years. I'm going to do the wrong thing for all the right reasons . . . just like my great-grandfather," he added, his voice hoarse with emotion.

"Maybe Captain Jonathan is trying to stop you from making the same mistake he did."

Wulff stared at her intently. "You don't really believe in stuff like that, do you?"

"Don't you?" she asked quietly.

"I'm not sure exactly what I believe right now. I'm a bit confused. No, I'm very confused."

"Can I help?" she asked, touching his forearm.

He covered her hand with his and smiled a soft, gentle smile that had a trace of pleading in it. "You sure can, sweetheart. If I think about this anymore tonight, I'll go crazy."

He lifted her hand and pressed it to his chest. "Touch me and take me away from it all. Make love to me, Brittany, please. Here, now."

Something in Wulff's eyes made her remember what he had said about losing his parents. He had been so young to be left alone in the world. And he had been alone ever since.

But Wulff was no longer a boy. Her hand slipped inside his shirt and ran along the warm, smooth skin of his chest, covered with the thick, silky hair of manhood. His body was that of a man's, but his eyes reflected a heart that still ached from loneliness.

She knew that he wasn't asking her for passion or lust. He needed to feel loved and cherished, the way that he had made her feel the first time they had made love.

One by one, her fingers opened the buttons of his shirt until she was able to pull the fabric aside and slip it off over his shoulders.

"You've made me feel so beautiful and special when you touched me, Aren," she said. "Now it's your turn."

She placed her hand on his chest and gently pushed him back onto the sand.

His smile was easy and relaxed as he lay, watching her. Only the accelerated thud of his heart beneath her hand betrayed his body's response to her touch.

She leaned down, kissed his lips and whispered, "Forget it all, Aren. Nothing matters tonight except you and me...and the way I'm going to make you feel."

Fascinated, she explored the varying textures of his body hair and the skin beneath it, which was as smooth as satin.

The hair on his chest narrowed to a line that disappeared into his jeans. Her hand followed its direction as she quickly loosed his belt and pulled down the zipper. In a moment she had removed his jeans and shoes.

She knelt beside him, glorying in the sight of him stretched out on the sand, nude except for a tiny pair of black briefs.

"Your body is magnificent," she murmured, running her hand over his vibrant skin, which glowed in the amber firelight. "I can't believe that it's all mine, to touch, to enjoy."

Groaning deep in his throat he reached for her, his hands moving to the edge of her shirt to lift it off.

Her hands captured his and returned them to his sides. "No," she said softly. "Let me do it for you. Let me do it all."

Slowly she pulled the shirt off over her head and cast it aside. She unclasped the front of her bra and pulled it away, tossing it on the sand beside the shirt. Her jeans quickly joined the pile of discarded garments.

His eyes were dark and heavy with desire as they followed her every movement, caressing her body as it was revealed to him.

Lying on the cool sand beside him, she draped one leg across his and delighted in the swell of his thigh muscles against her sensitive inner thigh.

A fine mist of ocean spray settled on their bare skin. Brittany shivered slightly and snuggled closer to his side, pressing her warm, full breast against his ribs. He moaned softly as she began a slow, thorough exploration of his body.

As she touched him Brittany realized why Wulff had made love to her so slowly. For the first time she understood the joy in knowing another person's body, completely and fully.

Her hands and lips moved over him, touching, tasting, savoring wonderful new discoveries, such as the tiny area just below his ear that radiated warmth from the pulse that throbbed there.

Her tongue found a deliciously silky spot in the crook of his elbow and another in the hollow below his collarbone.

She discovered that his nipples became taut peaks when her fingertips circled their sensitive edges and that his belly quivered when she trailed her long hair over its flat plane. She found that a delicate caress on his inner thigh brought a soft sigh from his lips.

She delighted in his deep groan of male satisfaction as her fingers slipped inside the black briefs and encircled his manhood.

Even more satisfying was the violent shudder that ran through his body when her lips and tongue joined her hands in drawing pleasure from the throbbing hardness.

"Oh God, Brittany," he groaned as his hands tangled themselves in her hair. "I want you."

"Now who's impatient?" she teased as she slowly pulled his briefs down over his legs and slipped out of her panties.

She moved over him, her knees on either side of his hips. His hands circled her waist as her fingers clutched his shoulders. Slowly she lowered herself onto him, guiding his rigid masculinity into her, filling her aching void.

As their bodies united, Brittany looked down into the face of the man she loved. Their eyes met and a bond was forged...a bond as timeless as the sea that surrounded them.

Wulff's body answered her primitive, sensuous rhythm. Around him, Wolf Island, the lighthouse and its history faded from his perception.

For those few brief moments his world narrowed down to that one patch of moonlit sand and the beautiful sea goddess who moved over him.

Her supple warmth stroked and caressed him until every nerve ending in his body screamed for release. Finally he felt a delicious shudder run through the slender form that he held in his hands. The last thing he saw was her gleaming body arching backward and the silver strands of her hair splayed against the moonlight as she threw back her head and cried out his name.

A second later even that vision disappeared as shock waves reverberated throughout his body and he closed his eyes, losing himself in a glorious oblivion.

"Aren? Are you all right?" a soft voice inquired anxiously.

"What? Oh, yes. I'm all right." He reached up and pulled her warm body down onto his. "In fact, I'm extremely all right." Wulff chuckled and tweaked her nose. "Hell, if I'd been any more all right I'd have died right here in your arms. It would have been terribly romantic, but not very practical."

"Shh." She covered his lips with her fingertips and glanced around anxiously. "You mustn't talk about dying, not here."

Wulff felt her shiver in his arms and saw the glint of tears in her eyes. He picked his shirt up from the sand, covered her with it and held her close to him.

"Hey, what is this, Nurse Brittany? Oh hell, I'm sorry, honey. I forgot that this is where—"

"It's not that." Tears traced silvery tracks down her cheeks.

"Then what is it, sweetheart?"

Brittany shuddered again and looked over her shoulder at the dark cove that glowed phosphorous blue in the light of the full moon. An ominous feeling crept over her, stealing away her peace and the sense of well-being their lovemaking had created. She felt the need to protect Wulff from a danger that she couldn't see and didn't understand.

"Oh, Aren, I couldn't bear to lose you." Her arms went around his neck in a strangling grip.

"You won't, love." He gently loosened her desperate hold and kissed her cheek. "You're just afraid because you lost your mother and Michael. But you're stuck with me. I'm not going anywhere. I promise."

Suddenly Brittany felt very cold. Her teeth began to chatter and her skin turned to gooseflesh. "Can we go back now? I don't feel good about being here in the cove anymore."

"Yes, of course," he said.

Wulff helped her dress and pulled on his jeans. Together they walked back up the path to the house.

Hours later, in the darkness of his bedroom, Wulff listened to the ship's bell chime away the early hours of the morning. Brittany's arm, which had gripped him tightly around his waist, had finally relaxed. She had fallen into a restless sleep.

He lay awake for another two hours, grappling with the most difficult decision of his life. As the first rays of dawn filtered through the window he, too, fell asleep.

Chapter Thirteen

Brittany approached the cottage's open door and peeked inside. The morning sun cast its golden beams through the one small window. She was surprised to see how much a bit of sunlight cheered the dismal cabin.

Jesse sat on one end of the threadbare sofa. In his lap was a large picture book and a napping Christopher Columbus, whose long ears draped over the boy's knee. Jesse's curly red head was bent over the book as he absorbed its brightly colored pages.

"Good morning, Jesse," she said, breaking his concentration.

"Oh, hi, Miss Davis. I didn't know you were there." He cast a furtive glance over at the bassinet and lowered his voice. "Shh…we have to be quiet. The baby's sleeping."

Brittany tiptoed over and looked down at the infant, who was snoring indelicately with his tiny fists curled contentedly on either side of his face.

She sat beside Jesse on the sofa and stroked the puppy's silky coat. "Where is everybody?"

"Granny's not up yet, and Deb's gone over to the store to get some stuff for breakfast," he whispered. "You said it was okay for her to take a walk if she felt like it, and she felt like it."

"So, you're left to baby-sit, huh?"

"Yep." He grinned proudly.

"If you want to go play, I'd be glad to watch him until Debra gets back."

Jesse looked wistfully out the window and then over at the bassinet. "That's okay," he said, unwilling to relinquish his post. "I'm his uncle. I'd better stick around."

Brittany smiled and closed his book so that she could see the cover. "Ah, *Walt Disney World*. Have you ever been there?"

"No. But, boy, I wish I could go. I bet it's the bestest place in the whole, wide world."

"You're absolutely right. It is," she replied, flipping through the pictures of Mickey Mouse, dancing dolls, singing bears, pillaging pirates and water spewing hippopotamuses.

"Have you been there?" he asked excitedly, forgetting his sleeping nephew.

"I sure have. Lots of times. I used to work there, a long time ago, when I was in college."

The boy's big eyes opened even wider as he surveyed Brittany with renewed respect. "Really? Oh, wow!" He glanced over her blond hair. "I'll bet you were Alice in Wonderland."

"No, nothing so glamorous, I'm afraid. I sold candy in the Candy Palace."

"But, still. Wow! Did you meet Mickey Mouse?"

"I sure did. I shared my coffee break with him several times."

Jesse was overcome by this added attraction. "Was Mickey nice?"

"Very nice," she assured him. "He likes kids."

"I knew it." The boy shook his head solemnly. "I knew that Mickey's nice and likes kids. Us kids know stuff like that. We can tell when people like us. I can tell that Mr. Wulff likes me, and I know you like me, too," he added shyly.

"Well, of course I do, Jesse. What's not to like? You're a charming fellow. In fact, you're my very favorite seven-year-old."

"Really?"

"Yep."

"Wow. If I'm your friend and you're Mickey's friend, then it's kinda like he's my friend, too. Right?"

"Absolutely."

Jesse slowly savored the thought. "Gee, wait till I tell the other kids. I need all the friends I can get, 'cause a lot of people don't like me."

Brittany studied the downcast eyes and bowed head. "Who doesn't like you, Jesse? The other kids?"

"Yeah. Some of them says I don't got a dad. But I do. I mean, I did. But he ran away 'cause he didn't like me. And my mom went to find him, but she didn't come back, 'cause she didn't like me neither. And Bob don't like me. He tells me to get lost all the time when I try to hang around with him."

Brittany wrapped her arm around the boy's frail shoulders and pulled him to her side. "Jesse, your parents didn't leave because of you. They had problems of their own that had nothing to do with you. And if people can't see what a special little boy you are, then there's something wrong with them, not you."

"Really?"

"Cross my heart."

"Hope to die?"

"Stick a needle in my eye."

"Ow." They both grimaced and snickered.

Jesse laid one grubby finger across her lips. "Shh. The baby."

A rustling at the door caught their attention, and they looked up to see Debra and Bob carrying baskets of fresh fruit and canned goods.

"What are you guys doing?" Debra asked. She handed her portion of the load to her cousin.

The acidic taste of bile rose in Brittany's throat as Bob brushed by her on his way to the tiny alcove that served as a kitchen in the back of the cabin. How could he look so harmless, so...nice, carrying Debra's groceries?

His freckled face was innocent, guileless. Brittany remembered her dream and the cold-blooded resolution that had shone in his eyes when he had held the stone over Michael.

"We're baby-sitting," she answered Debra, trying to keep the tension out of her voice.

"Looks to me like Jesse's boring you to death with his picture book. Mr. Wulff gave that to him on his birthday, and he's almost worn it out already."

"Uh-uh," Jesse argued. "I take care of my book and I took good care of the baby, too. See?"

Debra leaned over the bassinet and gathered the bundle expertly into her arms. Brittany noticed that the girl's awkwardness had disappeared, and she handled her baby with natural maternal ease.

"Did you miss me? I missed you," Debra cooed into the pink, shriveled face.

The baby answered with a lusty bawl.

"Yes, I thought you did," she said, settling into Granny's rocker and discreetly offering the child her breast.

"I see he's getting the hang of that," Brittany commented as the baby suckled noisily.

"He sure is. Have I told you that I decided on a name for him?"

"No, you haven't. What is it?"

Brittany thought she detected a slight flush among the freckles on the girl's face. "I thought I'd name him Aren Davis Wilson. Do you think that's okay?"

It was Brittany's turn to blush. "Okay? Why, that's nice. I'm terribly flattered and I'm sure Mr. Wulff will be, too. Thank you, Debra."

"I think we'll call him Davy," she said as the baby grasped her finger in his tiny fist.

Looking at the sprinkling of coppery fuzz on the infant's head, Brittany commented, "He looks like a Davy."

Bob stuck his head through the door. "Yeah, I told her to name it after me, but she wouldn't. See how she is?"

How can he do it? she thought. How can he stand there and joke and tease if he killed my brother? How can a murderer go on as though nothing has changed when he's taken someone's life?

"I'm not going to name my baby after a good-for-nothing bum like you," Debra was saying.

"Aw, you've been listening to Granny too long," he retorted. "Besides, what kind of thing is that to say to a guy who just put your groceries away for you? When are you gonna make my breakfast?"

"Your breakfast? Your breakfast is one of those grapefruits, and if Miss Davis wasn't here I'd tell you what you could do with it."

"Cranky, I tell you. She's still cr-a-nky."

Brittany noted that even though he spoke to her, his eyes carefully avoided her face.

She donned her thickest professional mask. "Debra needs all the rest she can get," she said pointedly.

"I know that. Gee, whiz, I was only kidding. I don't really expect her to cook for me."

"Since when," Debra muttered from the rocking chair.

Brittany breathed a sigh of relief as Bob crossed the small room to the door.

"I guess I'll leave if all I'm going to get around here is insults. And to think I was going to do a good deed tonight, too."

"A good deed? You?" his cousin asked sarcastically.

"Yeah. I was going to offer to watch the light for Wulff this evening so that he could take Miss Davis here over to Andros for a night on the town."

"How nice of you," Brittany replied evenly, thinking of what Wulff had told her about Bob's scheduled drug run.

She kept her gaze trained on Jesse's book, afraid that her face would betray her feelings if she looked up.

"Yeah, I've got some stuff to do earlier in the evening, but I'll be free later if you two feel like a little nightlife."

Brittany ventured a glance at him and saw that his fists were clenched tightly in his pockets and his body was tense, contrasting with the casual tone in his voice.

"Tell you what," he continued, staring at the linoleum, "you get all dressed up in something pretty and talk Wulff into taking you out. I'll show up later this evening."

"Thank you." Brittany's mouth smiled at him, but if Bob had not been avoiding her eyes, he would have looked into their icy depths and been chilled to the bone.

"I'll be sure to tell Aren. We'll be waiting for you."

As Brittany neared the top of the hill, she could feel that heavy, dark oppression steal over her again. She had temporarily escaped it in the village, but now that she had returned to Wolf Rock, the premonition was stronger than ever.

At first she had tried to tell herself that it was the fog that had settled over the island like a delicate, gray shroud. Instead of burning off as the sun rose in the sky, it became thicker and thicker. Its gossamer wisps floated among the tops of the palms and wrapped themselves like ghostly tentacles around the light tower.

As she climbed the stone stairs and stepped up onto the porch, Brittany could hear the muffled sound of angry male voices inside the house. She glanced down at the cove. The curtain of fog parted, and she saw an ugly green motorboat tied to the boat house dock. Evans.

She hesitated before opening the door. Maybe she should go for a long walk or something. No. If Wulff wanted her to leave, he would say so. And if Evans wanted her to leave—tough.

Opening the door, she heard the argument come to an abrupt halt. Evans stood in the middle of the living room. His ruddy face was flushed a livid purple, and his hands were perched on his fleshy, nondescript waist.

Before him stood Wulff, arms crossed defiantly across his broad chest. His expression was fixed in granite.

Evans glared at her. Obviously she was the last person in the world he wanted to see at that moment. He looked back at Wulff. "Well?" he demanded.

"Well what?"

"Are you going to tell her to leave or am I?"

Grinning, Wulff said, "Go ahead, but I'll warn you, she has a mind of her own, and she doesn't obey worth a damn."

Evans turned to Brittany. "Do you mind?" he asked sarcastically. "We have business to discuss that doesn't concern you."

"Really? I'd say that capturing the man who may have murdered my brother concerns me very much."

Evans's mouth fell open and Brittany thought of a landed carp. A fat, ugly, landed carp. "Wulff, you fool. You told her!" he shouted.

Aren's eyes narrowed to slits. "Watch who you're calling a fool," he growled. "Yes, I told her. I told her everything. She has a right to know what's going on."

"I don't believe this. You can't trust her. She's Davis's sister."

Wulff took a step toward Evans and Brittany thought he was going to strike him. "I trust her completely, and that's a hell of a lot more than I trust you. I'm not going to warn you again to watch your mouth. In fact, I think you'd better leave."

Evans stepped back, temporarily unnerved. When he recovered, he said, "I'm not leaving until we get this thing settled."

"You weren't listening. It is settled. I'm not turning out the light for any reason. If you can catch Bob with the dope some other way, more power to you. But the lamp stays lit."

"I don't understand why you're doing this," Evans blustered. "The man is garbage, a drug runner. He murdered your friend. Besides, I told you we'll fish him out of the water if he wrecks. We want to arrest him and seize the dope, not kill him."

Aren cast a sideways glance at Brittany, who stood tensely by his side. "And where have we heard this story before?" he muttered.

He looked back at Evans, his jaw tightly set. "The lamp stays lit," he repeated firmly.

"I can force you to cooperate. I'll get a court order to commandeer your light."

"Don't threaten me, Evans. And don't try to bluff me either. You don't have time to get any kind of order before tonight, and you aren't man enough to enforce one if you had it."

Wulff strode to the door and flung it open. "Get out of my house and off this rock. And don't let me see your ugly mug on my property again."

Fists clenched at his sides, Evans threatened, "You'll regret this, Wulff."

The light keeper opened the door wider. "I doubt it. Leave. Now."

Evans stomped through the doorway and disappeared down the steps. Wulff watched him long enough to see that he was heading toward the cove. Then he slammed the door and turned to Brittany.

"I'd be very glad to never see that bloody bugger again. God, he makes my flesh crawl."

"I know what you mean." She crossed the room to the sofa and sank into it. For the first time she realized that her knees were trembling. "I didn't like him when I first met him, and I like him even less now. I'm glad you decided not to go along with his plan."

"Are you, Brittany?" He sat on the sofa beside her and took her hand. "I didn't know how you'd feel about my decision."

"I wanted you to do what you thought was best. If Bob murdered Michael I want to see him punished. But I don't want you to turn out the light and regret it for the rest of your life the way Captain Jonathan did."

Wulff breathed deeply and wiped his palm across his forehead. "I hope that I won't regret letting Bob off the hook like this. I do believe in justice, you know."

"So do I. But you don't have to be its only instrument. A person's crimes have a way of coming back on him. Bob will pay for whatever he did, one way or the other."

"I certainly hope so. I couldn't go along with Evans's plan. It seemed all wrong somehow. Especially after finding Captain Jonathan's journal."

"By the way," she said, tracing her fingertip over the wolf's head on his arm. "Bob was at Debra's this morning, and I have a message for you from him."

"Oh, really? And what's that?"

"He offered to watch the light while you and I go over to Andros this evening for a bit of dining and dancing. Offered isn't quite the right word—insisted is more like it."

Wulff scowled. "He insisted that I go over to Nassau for some relaxation the night that Michael died.

What could he be up to this time? Evans said he's going to be making a run tonight. But he obviously wants us off the island.''

"He said he'd be busy earlier in the evening but he'll be by later.''

The lines in Wulff's face eased as the realization dawned on him. "Oh, okay. Now I know what he's doing. He wants to pick up the cocaine that he's got stashed here in the cove, and he wants us off the island so that we won't see him do it.''

"What cocaine?''

"The load that Michael was carrying when he wrecked. I'm pretty sure it's behind those rocks you spotted in the cave, the ones with the fresh scrapes on them. I figured he stashed it somewhere in the cove, but I didn't know where until you pointed out those stones to me.''

A grin spread slowly across Brittany's face. "Is that why you went to so much trouble to keep me from messing around with them?''

"One reason,'' he said, glancing at the bare length of her legs below her shorts. "Besides, if you're going to be messing around with something, I'd just as soon it was me.''

"So, what are we going to do?''

"About what?'' he asked, still distracted by her legs.

"About tonight.''

"Oh. Well, I'm not going to let Bob leave with that cocaine. If I do, he'll sell it in Miami for a fortune, and we'll never see his face around here again. I'm sure he figures that this is the big score he's been waiting for. And while I don't like the idea of him wrecking on the rocks, I don't want him to get away scot-free either.''

The premonition of disaster tightened its grip on Brittany's heart. "How are we going to stop him?"

Wulff smiled at her wrinkled frown. "We aren't; I am. Don't worry, Nurse Brittany. I outweigh him by nearly a hundred pounds. If all else fails, I'll sit on him."

"Don't joke about it. I'm worried about you."

He held her tightly against his side and pulled her head down onto his shoulder. "I know you are, love. But you don't need to be. I've been in a lot worse scrapes than this one. Didn't I ever tell you about that night over on Grand Bahama...?"

"Hot damn, Nurse Brittany, you look fantastic."

His gaze swept over her dress, taking in the lavender rosebud print and the delicate lacing down the front of its low-cut bodice. "I wish we were really going out tonight. You'd be delicious to cuddle up to on the dance floor."

"Then let's go, Wulff. Let's go to Andros," Brittany pleaded as she crossed the living room and stood beside him near the window.

"Come on, love. You don't mean that. You'd never forgive yourself if we let Bob go free."

"I've thought about it a lot. And I've decided I can live with that if I have to. But I don't want to live without you now that we're—"

"Ah, Brittany." He brushed a stray curl away from her face. "We're not going to go into that again, are we? Bob will be here any minute. I've stashed our jeans, shirts and sneakers in the boat, and we're ready to go through with this. Have a little faith and it'll all work out. Okay?"

Brittany slipped her hands beneath his white, linen jacket to embrace him. She jumped when her hand brushed a hard, cold bulk that was thrust into the waistband of his slacks.

"Aren?" Her voice trembled.

"My father's service revolver. Don't worry. I know how to use it if I have to."

She wrapped her arms around his waist, avoiding the gun. As she held him tightly, she tried to banish the thought that it might be the last time.

The bell on the porch pealed and she felt him tense in her arms.

"Can you do this?" he asked anxiously.

She nodded and reluctantly withdrew from him, allowing him to answer the door.

Bob entered the house and looked relieved when he saw Aren's jacket and slacks. "Hey, you're all dressed up. You must have decided to accept my offer."

A wry smile curled Wulff's lips. "An evening away from the light with a beautiful lady is hard to refuse."

"Good. You deserve it. The fog's getting pretty thick. I'll go on up and keep watch. You kids have a good time and don't hurry back. Spend the night if you want."

Wulff's face was an inscrutable mask as he draped Brittany's sweater over her shoulders.

"We might just do that," he said smoothly. "Thanks, Bob."

Wulff looked squarely into his eyes. The younger man glanced away uncomfortably, and Brittany remembered how soul piercing those pale blue eyes were. It was difficult to hide anything from Aren Wulff.

Bob cleared his throat and headed toward the kitchen and the back door. "Well, have a good time. See ya later."

"Sooner than you think, old chap," Wulff muttered in a low, ominous tone. "Much sooner than you think."

"Is he up there? Do you see anything?" The toe of her sneaker sought a firmer hold among the loose rocks of the cliff.

Wulff lowered the binoculars and surveyed the moonlit cove below. "It's hard to see anything through this fog, but I don't think he's in the light anymore. He must have left as soon as our boat was out of sight. I had a feeling he would."

"Maybe we were gone too long." Brittany consulted her watch. "It's been over a half hour."

He leaned forward and rested his body against the stones at the top of the ridge. "I know, but we had to get far enough away that he couldn't see us. He was watching like a hawk from the light when we left."

"So, where do you think he is now?"

"I don't know. He could already be in the cave, I suppose. What's the matter, love? Are you cold?"

Brittany clenched her teeth together tightly to keep them from chattering. "No. I guess it's an adrenaline rush. I don't usually shake like this under stress."

Wulff slipped his hand beneath her hair and lightly massaged her neck. "This isn't the kind of stressful situation that you're accustomed to handling, is it, Nurse Brittany?"

"No, it isn't. Capturing murderers and drug runners wasn't part of my medical training." Her eyes searched his face. "Are you scared?" she asked.

He thought for a moment, then said, "Not exactly scared, more excited and anxious to get this over with."

Yes, by this time tomorrow night it would be over, finished. She looked at Wulff standing beside her, strong, healthy, whole. This time tomorrow night would he still be vibrant . . . and alive? Or would he be another restless spirit haunting Wolf Cove, crying out for vengeance?

She looked down at the cave entrances, a trio of black arches against the dark blue of the cliffs surrounding the cove. Overhead the full moon's outline was diffused by the ever thickening haze of fog that drifted across its face.

A phosphorous sheen of moonlight dimly lit the scene. The drifting fog gave Wolf Cove a surrealistic, dreamlike quality.

Dreamlike? No, Brittany thought as an icy wave of foreboding swept over her. Not a dream—a nightmare.

In the pale moonlight the wolf waited with gaping, foaming jaws and pointed fangs. Waited to devour its living prey.

A deep-throated roar shattered the stillness. The blast vibrated through Brittany's body, jarring her senses. She grabbed at Wulff as she lost her footing.

He pulled her to her feet and clasped her to his chest. The sound stopped as suddenly as it had begun. He laughed softly into her hair and said, "What's the matter, Nurse Brittany? Haven't you ever heard a foghorn?"

"Yes, but I've never felt one before. Good heavens, that thing is loud. My ears are still ringing."

His hands tightened around her waist. "That's not your ears ringing," he said, lowering his voice. "That's a boat motor. And it's coming this way. Get down."

They crouched behind the ragged edge of the cliff and watched. A speedboat, sleek and latently powerful, crept through the black waters of the cove, carefully choosing its way among the glistening teeth of the wolf. The driver slowly maneuvered the craft to the beach in front of the largest cave.

"Is it Bob?" Brittany whispered.

"Yep." Wulff stared through the binoculars. "It's just as we thought. He's after the cocaine. He thinks he's going to get away with the stuff he's running, Michael's load, plus over a hundred grand worth of speedboat." He lowered the binoculars and slowly shook his head. "Not bad for one night's work."

"And one murder," she added grimly.

"There he goes."

Bob slipped a backpack on his shoulders and jumped over the side of the boat into waist-high water. He lifted something from the stern and carried it to the shore.

"What's he doing?" she asked as the thin figure on the beach leaned over and stuck the object he was carrying into the silver sand.

"He's anchoring the boat so that it doesn't drift while he's in the cave."

"Okay, what do we do now?" she asked breathlessly as their quarry disappeared into the largest of the black holes in the cliff.

When another blast from the foghorn subsided, he replied, "I'm going to go down there and wait for him to come out."

He flexed his stiff muscles and handed her the binoculars. "You stay here. Don't worry. This won't take long."

"I'm going with you," she said as he began his descent over the rocks.

"No, you aren't. I brought you along as a witness. Now get back behind those rocks and witness."

"I'm going with you," she repeated gently but firmly. This was one battle she couldn't afford to lose.

Wulff sighed in exasperation. "This is no time for an argument."

"You're right. It isn't. Let's go."

He grabbed her waist as she stumbled down the rocks beside him. "Damn it, Brittany. Could you do as you're told this once? I don't want you to get hurt."

She blinked her eyes against the image of her brother bleeding, dying on the white sand of Wolf Cove. She had lost Michael. She couldn't lose Aren. "I keep telling you, I'm not the one in danger tonight. You are."

Even in the dim light she could see anger glittering in his eyes as he glared at her. "I'm supposed to let you go down there because you have some kind of... of... premonition?"

"Yes. It's a strong one. I know I'm right."

Wulff glanced down at the black arch in the cliff and back at her. They were wasting precious time and they both knew it. "Let's hope you're right," he said. "I'll never forgive myself if anything happens to you. Come on."

They scrambled as quietly as possible down the cliff to the beach. When they neared the cave entrance, he laid a finger across his lips and motioned for her to position herself on one side of the opening behind a large rock. He backed against the wall on the opposite side.

An eternity ticked by as they waited. The insidious fog twined its feathery, gray wisps around them. The horn sounded intermittent blasts. Far above them Wolf Light's beam pierced the darkness.

Brittany wiped her palms on her thighs. She inhaled deeply. There was death in the air tonight. She could feel it . . . smell it . . . taste it.

They heard a rustling inside—Bob was coming out.

He cautiously exited the cave and glanced nervously about him, his eyes searching the cove.

Although she was watching for it, her eye hardly caught Wulff's move when he made it. In a split second the keeper had grabbed his assistant with his left hand and twisted his arm behind his back. Wulff's right hand held the revolver against the base of Bob's skull.

"What the hell?" the redhead shouted in surprise as he craned his neck to see who held him. "Wulff! I thought—"

"I know what you thought, friend." Wulff's voice was low and deadly. "You thought you'd get rid of me, desert my light and take off with your backpack full of goodies."

"I don't know what you're talking about," he protested, trying to twist out of the light keeper's grip.

"Then why don't we open your little knapsack here and see what's for dinner."

Brittany watched tensely as Wulff released Bob's arm and pulled the heavy pack from his shoulders. He lifted the flap and looked inside.

"Well, what have we here? A knapsack full of cocaine. That would have set you up in style for a few years. Too bad you're not going to get the chance to cash in on it.''

''What are you going to do with me?'' Bob's voice was high, thin, desperate.

''I'm going to take you to New Providence and turn you over to the authorities. Put your hands behind your back.''

Reluctantly Bob complied with Wulff's order. ''Why? What the hell is it to you anyway? Why do you care?''

''Why do I care? Don't you think it matters to me if you walk out of here a rich, free man? You killed my friend.'' Wulff glanced over at Brittany, who had left her hiding place behind the rock. ''You murdered the brother of the woman I love. You don't really think I'm going to let you get away with that, do you?''

''How...how did you know?'' Bob sputtered.

Brittany felt an icy fist close around her heart. It was true. Her brother had been murdered, senselessly, brutally.

''I didn't know for sure,'' Wulff replied, ''until now. There's nothing like a confession for proof.''

The keeper backed several paces away from his captive. With his left hand he reached into his pocket and produced a roll of black electrical tape. He muttered a curse as he fumbled, trying to unwind a length of the sticky tape with one hand while holding the gun on Bob with the other.

''Here, let me do that.'' Brittany hurried to him and reached for the roll in his hand.

He hesitated, then relinquished his hold on the tape.

''All right, but watch yourself,'' he warned, ''and stay out of my line of fire.''

Cautiously she approached Bob's back. She saw him tremble and sensed his terror, like that of a trapped animal. The smell of his sweat was rank and sour.

She unrolled the black tape and reached for his hands. Long, thin hands. Hands that had killed her brother.

The moment the tape touched his skin he jerked as though she had shocked him with a live wire. As though in slow motion, she saw the bony hand reach for her...grab her arm...and pull her toward him. Before she had time to think, let alone react, her body was a shield between him and Wulff's revolver.

Bob's hand moved to his waist. A gun materialized. Cold steel glinted in the moonlight. He pointed the revolver at Wulff. The light keeper's eyes narrowed as he looked from the gun to his assistant.

"Come on, Bob. I've known you all your life. You're not going to kill me. Now put that thing down before somebody gets hurt."

Bob's arm shook violently as it tightened around Brittany's waist. His shallow chest heaved with ragged gasps against her side.

"I don't want to hurt you, Wulff. Give me the pack and I'll get out of here. You'll never see me again. That's all I want."

Wulff took one step toward him, but stopped when Bob cocked the hammer of the revolver and pointed it at Brittany. The steel barrel jabbed painfully into her cheek.

She wanted to jerk her face away, but cold logic froze her. She mustn't move. Mustn't even breathe. His hand was shaking so badly that any movement at all could—

"That's far enough, Wulff," he panted. "You've got what I want and I've got what you want. Throw down your gun and we'll trade."

"If you hurt that girl, Bob, I swear I'll kill you," the light keeper ground out, his voice thick with rage.

"I won't hurt her if you do what I say. Throw down your gun and toss the pack over here. Then I'll let her go."

The booming sound of the foghorn jarred their already strained nerves. Wulff reluctantly dropped the revolver into the sand and threw the backpack at Bob's feet.

"There, you've got your bloody dope. Now let her go, and get the hell out of here."

Bob released his grip on Brittany and she quickly stepped away from him. Wulff pulled her to his side.

Warily Bob backed away from them, keeping his gun trained on Wulff. He clumsily hefted the pack onto his shoulders and tightened the straps across his chest.

Brittany slowly expelled the breath that she had been holding. Maybe . . . just maybe . . .

Out of the corner of her eye she saw a flurry of activity on the cliffs behind Bob. Half a dozen men hurried down the rocks toward them. When they drew closer, she recognized one of them as Evans.

Bob saw them, too. She heard his gasp of surprise and dismay as he watched the group descend on him. His eyes darted back to Wulff. Rage contorted his face.

"You turned me in!" he shouted. "Damn you, I worked for you and you turned me in!"

Brittany watched in horror as the expressions of fear and indecision crossed his face. She had seen those looks before. She knew what they meant.

Even more familiar and terrifying was the cold-blooded resolution in his eyes. His finger tightened on the trigger.

Once again Brittany tried to throw herself between the murderer and a man she loved. Once again she was too late.

"No!" she screamed. The gun's blast rent the air. Its fire flashed in the darkness. She choked on the acidic smoke.

The light keeper's body reeled from the impact of the bullet, and he crumpled into a heap on the beach.

"Wulff!" She threw herself over him, her hand covering the dark hole. His blood welled between her fingers and stained the white sand.

A hand grabbed her arm and yanked her to her feet. She was dragged along the beach, toward the water...away from Wulff.

"No!" she cried, plowing her feet into the soft sand. "Let me go! He's bleeding. He'll die if I don't help him!"

"He's already dead. Come on." He jerked her arm so hard that it was nearly torn from its socket. A red-hot pain shot through her shoulder.

"Stay back," she heard her captor shout. "Stay away or she gets it too."

She had a vague impression of Evans and his men standing on the beach, guns drawn impotently.

Bob pulled her into the water with him. It was warm, like bathwater. Such a strange thought at a time like this, she mused. With Wulff bleeding, into the sands. Dying. Without her.

Something snapped inside her. Sanity fled. A savage cry exploded out of her chest. She launched herself at him. Her nails clawed his face, tearing at the tender flesh, groping for his eye sockets. Her knee pistoned upward and slammed into his groin.

His breath left his body in a scream of agony. "You bitch!" he shrieked.

Brittany saw more than felt the pain when the steel revolver struck the side of her head. Bright, sparkling colors swirled through her brain and across her eyes, blotting out her thoughts, her vision.

Then, even the sparkling kaleidoscope of color faded. She felt herself sinking into the warm, liquid blackness. Saltwater seared her throat, nose and lungs. She tried to swim, but the water was so thick, and her arms were too heavy.

Someone was lifting her, pulling her up by her long hair. "Not yet," she heard him say. "I'm not done with you yet. Get in!"

He grabbed her hips and boosted her over the side of the boat. She fell heavily facedown on the deck. Sputtering, choking, she gasped for breath. The pain in her head roared, drowning out all other sensations, even the fire in her throat and lungs.

Bob followed her into the boat, his ascent more difficult because of the heavy pack strapped to his back.

Crouching low, he hurried to the wheel and turned the key. The powerful engine roared to life. He threw the speedboat into reverse. Brittany had struggled to her hands and knees but was thrown on her side as the craft lurched beneath her.

They had only gone thirty feet when the engine whined and ground to a halt. Bob scrambled to the stern, keeping his body low and out of range of the agents' guns.

Simultaneously Brittany crawled to the back of the boat and pulled herself up until she could see over the edge.

Bob bent down and swore vehemently. His forgotten anchor line was hopelessly tangled in the propeller blades. He leaned over the edge to tug at the nylon rope. As his hand reached downward, the water below him became unnaturally still. Brittany could see clearly his face and outstretched hand reflected in the mirrored surface.

Just before his hand touched the water, it seemed to Brittany that the reflection became distorted. Her throbbing head and teary eyes made it difficult to see... to think.

She blinked and watched as the features in the water changed. The image with its outstretched hand was no longer Bob's.... It was Michael's.

Golden eyes burned with fiery rage as the reflected hand met the assistant's flesh and blood at the water's surface.

Brittany heard her own screams mix with Bob's as he tumbled headlong into the black waters of the cove.

Chapter Fourteen

Leaning back against the tower, Brittany stretched her legs, closed her eyes and inhaled the sea breeze caressing her face. She opened her eyes and looked down at the cove. For the first time since she had seen it the place appeared restful, serene and content. The victims of Wolf Cove were at peace. The ultimate price had been paid.

"Well, love, does the place feel better to you now?"

She looked over at Wulff, who sat watching her, his pale blue eyes reaching into her soul. "Yes, it feels better now," she replied simply.

"So, you accomplished what you came here to do. You fulfilled your brother's dream, and now you can put his memory to rest once and for all."

"Yes. I'm glad it's over, all except for the nightmares."

"Are you still having those?"

"Yes, but not as often as I did right after—" She gulped painfully.

Wulff's hand closed over hers. "I'm sorry that was such a terrible experience for you, sweetheart. I'll never forgive Bob for putting you through that."

"Yes, well, Bob paid for what he did."

"He certainly did. His greed got him in the end. That backpack dragged him right down."

"He was dragged down all right." Brittany remembered the reflection in the water and shuddered. Had she really seen Michael's face? Or had it been the stress of seeing Wulff shot and the trauma of having been assaulted?

"I wish that you hadn't been hurt," she said.

Wulff looked down at the white sling that supported his arm. "Oh, it wasn't all that bad. It hardly hurts at all anymore. Besides, I've enjoyed all the attention I've received these last few weeks at the hands of a certain pretty nurse with great bedside manners."

She laughed and squeezed the rough hand that held hers. "Well, you've been a lousy patient. I told you to take it easy, and you went traipsing off to Nassau and Miami. I swear, you would have helped those guys load the guns if I hadn't sat on you."

Wulff's eyes twinkled at the memory of how easily she had lured him from the cove up to the house. "Yeah, that was fun. You'll have to 'sit' on me again sometime."

He laughed as he watched the pink flush stain her cheeks.

"Thank you again, Aren, for selling those guns for me. I wouldn't have known where to begin. And you must have driven a hard bargain to get as much as you did from that dealer."

"You've already thanked me a dozen times. I was glad to do it."

Brittany cleared her throat. She decided to launch into the subject that she had been saving for the right time. "Ah, Wulff, there's something I want to tell you."

"I was wondering when you were going to get around to it. Go on...."

"I've been thinking about what I should do. And now that you're stronger, I need to go back to Orlando—"

"I understand," he interrupted. He lowered his head, but not before she saw the pain in his eyes.

"No, I don't think you do."

"Sure. You've got enough money now to do anything you've ever wanted, and you should be getting on with your life. I can't expect you to stay cooped up here on this island with me forever."

Brittany moved closer to him and placed her finger on his lips. "Shh...hush. Don't say another word until you hear what I have to say."

Her arms went around his neck, and her fingers toyed with the dark curls on his collar. "I don't want to leave Wolf Island. I love you and Jesse and Debra. I want to stay here for the rest of my life and watch Jesse and little Davy grow into men. If I leave now, I'll never know what Christopher Columbus will look like when he's full grown."

Wulff's hand lifted her chin and his eyes searched hers. "Do you really mean that?"

"Absolutely."

"Then what did you mean about going back to Orlando?"

"I have to tie up some loose ends before I can move down here. It'll only take a couple of weeks. I have to clear out my apartment, and I have some special shopping to do now that I'm loaded with cash."

He grinned and tweaked her nose. "And what are you going to buy? You said you don't like diamonds or furs."

She gave him her most beguiling smile. "I have to find out how a rich woman finances the building of a modest clinic and school on a small island. I'm sure there must be a contractor in Orlando, Miami or Nassau who can handle the project. I'm going to get him to throw in a couple of extra bedrooms for Debra and Jesse while he's at it."

Wulff stared at her, a mixture of astonishment and tenderness on his face. "Are you sure that's how you want to spend your money?"

"Can you think of a better way?"

Tears clouded his eyes as he lifted her hand and kissed its palm. "No, love, I can't."

"Neither can I. Besides, I have an ulterior motive. I'm buying myself a job that I'll love. With a well-stocked clinic I'll be able to provide proper health care for the people on the island. And I figure there will be enough money left to lure a good teacher for the school from Andros or New Providence. What do you think?"

"I think you're a hell of a fine woman, Nurse Brittany," he said, his voice husky. "When are you figuring on doing all of this?"

"As soon as your arm heals and you find someone to watch the light for a couple of weeks. I want to take you with me. I can use your good business head while I'm dealing with the contractor and besides..." She smiled shyly. "I'd love to show you off to the other nurses at the hospital when I tell them goodbye."

It was Wulff's turn to blush. "Well, I don't know about that. But I'd like to go along with you. I haven't been to Orlando for years. It's a beautiful city, a nice place for a honeymoon."

Brittany caught her breath. "A honeymoon?"

"Yeah, you know, like after you get married, you go on a trip and fool around a lot and—"

"I know what a honeymoon is. But you've never said, I mean, I didn't know you wanted to...I mean."

Wulff stifled her babbling with a soft kiss. "Nurse Brittany, will you marry me?" he asked, running his fingers through her hair and along her cheek. "There's a minister in the village who can perform the ceremony. We'll tie the knot right here in the top of the light. Jesse can stand up with me and Debra could for you, and we can crowd as many of the villagers as possible into the chamber and around the balcony—"

"Wait. Wait a minute. Are you sure?"

"Sure that I want you? Ah, yes, love, very sure. How about you?"

Brittany looked into his eyes and saw the future. She saw a hoard of "dirty little bilge rats" on Wulff's knees and at his feet listening to *Treasure Island*. She saw leisurely walks along the beach at sunset and picnics on the balcony, fulfilled days of nursing and long nights in Wulff's arms.

"Oh, yes, I'm sure, too. There's just one thing," she said, pulling back as he lowered his head to kiss her.

"And what's that?" He planted the kiss on her nose.

"I know it's not very romantic to take along an extra person on your honeymoon. But could we please take Jesse to Orlando with us? I want to show him Walt

Disney World, and there's a friend of mine there I want to introduce him to."

"Whatever you say, Nurse Brittany." He sighed as his hand moved over her chest, loosening the buttons on her blouse. How could he deny this woman anything?

Wulff felt a delicious heaviness building in his loins as his fingers slipped inside her shirt and found the exquisite softness of her breast.

His lips brushed over hers lightly before following the trail his fingers had blazed. "But if we're going to take Jesse on our honeymoon, we'd better start the fooling around part right now...."

"But your arm," she protested as he pulled her across his lap.

"That's all right, love," he murmured, "I have another...."

DOUBLE JEOPARDY—Brooke Hastings
Ellie came to Raven's Island to take part in a romantic mystery-adventure game but soon found herself caught in the middle of a real romance and a real adventure where murder wasn't just a game.

SHADOWS IN THE NIGHT—Linda Turner
When Samantha was kidnapped, she knew there was little hope for her unless the handsome dark-haired smuggler risked his place in the gang and his life to help her escape.

WILDCATTER'S PROMISE—Margaret Ripy
Financially, Cade was a gambler, but emotionally he was afraid to risk anything. Kate had to convince him to take that one extra step and fill the void in their lives.

JUST A KISS AWAY—Natalie Bishop
At first it was a case of mistaken identities, but Gavin soon realized that Callie was the woman he should have been searching for all along.

OUT OF A DREAM—Diana Stuart
Tara and Brian were both trying to escape, and their chance encounter on Cape Cod was perfect, the stuff out of fantasies. But could the romance last when real life intruded? They had to find out.

WHIMS OF FATE—Ruth Langan
Kirsten couldn't forget the mysterious stranger who had stolen a kiss.... He was prince of the country and heir to the throne, and Cinderella is only a fairy tale. Isn't it?

AVAILABLE NOW:

A WALK IN PARADISE
Ada Steward

EVERY MOMENT COUNTS
Martha Hix

A WILL AND A WAY
Nora Roberts

A SPECIAL MAN
Billie Green

ROSES AND REGRETS
Bay Matthews

LEGACY OF THE WOLF
Sonja Massie